P9-ECU-754

BLOOD MOON

BLOOD MOON

A. W. Gryphon

Sense of Wonder Press
JAMES A. ROCK & COMPANY, PUBLISHERS
ROCKVILLE • MARYLAND

Blood Moon by A. W. Gryphon

SENSE OF WONDER PRESS
is an imprint of JAMES A. ROCK & CO., PUBLISHERS

Cover photograph copyright ©2008 by A. W. Gryphon.
*Fountain sculpture by William McMillan, located outside
The National Gallery, London, Trafalgar Square.*

Address comments and inquiries to:
SENSE OF WONDER PRESS
James A. Rock & Company, Publishers
9710 Traville Gateway Drive, #305
Rockville, MD 20850
E-mail:
jrock@rockpublishing.com   lrock@rockpublishing.com
Internet URL: www.rockpublishing.com

ISBN: 978-1-59663-609-5 / 1-59663-609-2

Library of Congress Control Number: 2007933894

Printed in the United States of America

First Edition: 2008

For Lucy and Mildred

Each year, as the world passes through the Autumnal Equinox, we enter the month of October and the cycle of the Blood Moon. Also known as the Hunter's Moon, it is a moon of new goals, protection, spirituality and resolution. It represents a time of transition, when the leaves fall and the earth is bare. When fields have been reaped and it becomes time to take on the hunt as our means of sustenance ... and it becomes time to settle the past ... and it becomes time to honor life's purpose, and to honor love's truth, and to know the true power of the Witch.

Witch: A craftsperson of magick. One who uses magick, i.e. Witchcraft or The Craft, in their every day life.

Wicca: An earth-based religion, with Pagan roots, practiced by most, but not all, Witches and by many common men and women.

PROLOGUE

In the early 1400s, among many religions and beliefs, the practice of Wicca and Witchcraft had come to flourish in Europe. The typical Witch was peaceful, using his or her abilities to give back to the earth and its inhabitants. Most Wiccans belonged to a Coven and each Coven was guided by a High Priest and a High Priestess; neither the superior, they were together as one. The most famous of the Wiccans were the Celtic High Priest Domhall (DUN-nal) and the Celtic High Priestess Maeve (MAVE), a husband and wife, both born with strong and pure powers combined with the natural ability to lead, teach and execute magick. Their reputation was known throughout the continent.

Witches and Wiccans lived peacefully alongside common men until the late 1400s when the reign of Pope Innocent VIII began. He followed in the footsteps of his predecessors, starting with Pope Gregory I, by continuing the Christianization of Europe, uniting Church and State and advising the people, peasants, noblemen and otherwise, on the evils of the Witches. He did not differentiate between those who only practiced Wicca, Witches who practiced Wicca and Witches who practiced only their craft. They were all simply, "Witches" under his rule.

In speaking out against the Witches, the Pope was also able to *put women in their place,* so to speak; something that was necessary in the mind of both the Church and government. In old-world Europe, women had been considered equal. Under the government supported Church, an independent woman was a Witch of evil intent and punishable by death. It was a time of manipulation, deception, control and chaos, and it was only the beginning.

In 1484 the Pope wrote a letter to the people explaining the evils and dangers of the Witches, and how to deal with them. He called for their conversion or removal at any cost. The Pope's message was heard far and wide with the help of new technology, the printing press, which provided the ability to replicate and distribute his letter in massive quantities.

The Pope's credo, inspired the *Malleus Malleficarium* or *Witches Hammer* written by Heinrich Kramer and Jakob Sprenger, two German monks. A book that came to be accepted as the official "Witch Hunter's Manual." Its mass distribution and the Pope's letter led to what has become known as "The Burning Times," when it has been estimated that over a million accused Witches were hung, burned, tortured, or stoned to death. Because of this, thousands of Witches converted to Christianity purely out of fear for their lives and those of their families.

To further the threat against Witches, a right-wing group of self-appointed Witch hunters calling themselves "The Organization" formed and did not bother attempting to convert anyone. They believed all Witches to be against God and the cause of the world's plagues. Their purpose was to seek and destroy. These men were feared far more than the Church or the State and, unofficially, those bodies supported The Organization, both financially and in spirit. Because of The Organization, very few Witches dared to stand their ground and defend their beliefs. The famous High Priest Domhall and High Priestess Maeve were among those who did. They agreed to wage a war, endangering their lives, those of their followers and that of the baby the High Priestess Maeve was carrying in her womb. They believed that, in the end, the power of pure goodness came from the power that created the universe and eventually it would overcome any man-made evil.

Not long after the wars against The Organization and The Church began, all of those still dedicated to The Craft and the beliefs of Wicca gathered for a special and sacred celebration. It was October 31, Samhain (SOW-in), the Pagan New Year. It was a unique night because that year October's Full Blood Moon and Maeve's twenty-eighth birthday fell on the same night as Samhain.

Almost one-hundred Witches gathered at Stonehenge for the occasion, but none of them knew just what the night would bring.

Samhain is the one day each year when the natural order of the universe reverts to undefined chaos so that we can move on from the past and establish new order for the year to come. It is a night that exists outside of time, in which the lands of the dead and those of the living come together as one and the spirits roam the world among the mortals for a celebration of the past and the betterment of the future.

A woman's twenty-eighth birthday represents the beginning of her fourth and, what most consider, her most powerful cycle in her seven year cycles of life. The fact that the twenty-eighth birthday of the High Priestess fell on this day was sacred, but what happened on that particular night, when the moon was closest to the earth and glowed like red fire, is what set in motion a cycle of events that would change the course of The Craft forever.

At the peak of the ceremony, when the High Priestess had embodied the Ancient Celtic Goddess Brigid in celebration of the night, she let out a cry and fell to the ground. She crawled to the center of the ceremony circle with the help of another woman. The Coven stood in silence watching her, afraid to interfere, unsure of what was happening.

Maeve was in labor. She was two months premature, but the baby was coming quickly. In a matter of minutes a little girl was born. The woman assisting in the birth wrapped the child in a cloth and placed her in the proud High Priest's arms, just in time for Maeve to scream again. The woman rushed back over to her. She placed her hand on Maeve's belly and looked to The Coven, then to Domhall. There was a second child coming. A twin. She had no sooner announced it, when the child pushed through. In an unworldly and quickened moment, the High Priestess gave birth to a son. Domhall and The Coven were overcome with emotion. They could not help, but *know,* that this was a sign not only from the God and the Goddess, but from The All.

It was a sign so significant that it triggered something unexpected in the High Priest. It brought out a previously unknown darkness, lurking deep in his soul. For the sake of Wicca's future, he declared the war would be taken to another level. For the good purpose of destroying those who threatened the Witches' way of life, The Coven would open themselves to their dark side within and fight the opposition with an evil intent that matched theirs. They would fight so that one day the twins would be free just as they once were. The High Priest handed his daughter to his wife then he took his son and raised him high in the air, cheering his new declaration, "An eye for an eye!"

Maeve was horrified by her husband's turn. Evil was not their way, it never had been; but it took only a moment for her to see that something had changed in him that night. Something that could not be reversed. As he, again, raised their newborn son in the air and called out for an attack of magick on The Church and The Organization, the High Priestess and twelve followers took the baby girl and ran off into the night, terrified, but unnoticed in the frenzy the High Priest had created.

From then on, not only did the wars between the Witches and The Organization and the Witches and the government controlled Church continue, the High Priest waged a Civil War on all Witches who chose not to fight under his directives, who he claimed were deserters. In actuality, it was not only that they had deserted him that infuriated the High Priest, but that Domhall's power was cut in half by losing his wife. She was the only one whose natural abilities exactly matched his. Natural abilities that made her a perfect ally or an undefeatable enemy.

Maeve and Domhall never saw each other again. The High Priestess raised their daughter. She named her Cathal Eimhin (KAhul Ay-veen), which means prompt, ready and strong in battle. She taught her to be a pure Witch of good, and to fight all three wars, but only by the spread of positive forces and the faith of Wicca.

The High Priest named their son Budahach (BOO-ach), meaning victorious. He taught him the forces of evil and the craft of black magick. Budahach was trained to channel his magickal abilities so that he could fight the wars without respecting the universal balance on which Wiccans believe The Craft rests. Domhall taught Budahach to break the basic and virtually only rule of Wicca, "Do Not Bring Harm Onto Others." This made them men of evil, men who the Wiccans believed were unworthy of calling themselves "Witches" at all.

Domhall and his followers had broken the laws of Wicca, but they were still Witches and Witches with belief in their own good intentions. Domhall and his followers had always practiced Wicca. They believed that the changes in their ways were not evil, but a necessary evolution in the changed times with which they were faced. They declared themselves Witches of a new philosophy, but Witches none-the-less. No one dared challenge their position. No one other than the High Priestess. The Organization didn't care, nor did the Church or government, and the elders of Wicca who'd hidden in the woods to live out their lives, their way, had all become too fearful to be involved in taking sides or proactively making any wrongs right. A Witch was a Witch and a Christian was a Christian. That was the new way and those who wanted a chance at survival would accept that.

The High Priest became so consumed by his determination to win the wars and pursue victory that, to ensure success in future conflicts, he placed a spell on his son. The result of this spell was that all the children to follow in his son's bloodline would be instilled with the power and rage necessary to continue the war against The Organization, against the Church, and against the opposing Witches, for as long as the battles continued.

Budahach and Cathal were two children with identical and pure power; they were twins, but complimentary opposites. Others would follow, but it would be their bloodline that remained the strongest among the Witches and it would be the division of that bloodline that would keep the opposition parallel. Because they were equal to such a degree, the only entity that could redirect what had been done was the universe itself. A stronger child needed creating and that was something which would happen naturally in time with the cycles of the universe.

One day, far beyond the lifetimes of Budahach and Cathal, the wheel of time would bring the universe back to a similar night.

The planets would again align with the seven-year cycle of a female Witch from the bloodline created by the High Priest and High Priestess. That woman's twenty-eighth birthday would fall on Samhain, under a Full Blood Moon and on that night, when the moon came closest to earth, she would be infused with "The Ultimate Power." She would be as pure as the twins with their strength combined; strong enough, both spiritually and physically, to overcome her distant magick relative, The Organization and any other opposition that faced what she stood for.

For hundreds of years tales were spun, stories were written and prophecies were told in anticipation of the inevitable, the coming of a girl who would come to be known as "The One."

PART ONE

chapter 1

San Francisco, California
September 22, 1984 — Mabon

Amongst the tall trees and midnight shadows playing off the Full Moon in San Francisco's Golden Gate Park, thirteen members of the Wiccan faith joined together for the celebration of Mabon. As the final cycle in the eight-tiered wheel of the Pagan year, Mabon is a time of death and re-birth, of growth and reflection, and most important to the practitioners of Wicca and Witchcraft, a time of balance.

The Coven, made up of five women, five men, one boy and seven-year-old Amelia Pivens, stood in a circle, facing each other. On the ground, in the center of the circle, was a pentagram fashioned out of dried corn stalks to represent the harvest. Brown candles marked the west side of the circle and white marked the east. The brown represented a farewell to the past and the white stood for The Coven's embrace of the days to come.

Amelia's mother, Grace, stepped outside the circle and wrapped both of her hands around a ritual dagger with a six inch blade and a six inch bone handle, called an athame (AH-tha-my). She raised it toward the North Star then walked around The Coven creating a Circle of Protection; a Circle that would protect The Coven from any outside influences, dangers or negative energy. When Grace completed the Circle, she joined hands with The Coven and they all closed their eyes. Grace first called on the Quarters for protection. She called to the angels: Uriel to protect the north side of the Circle; Raphael to protect the east; Michael for the south; and Gabriel for the west.

She chose the angels that night not because they were her first choice, but because she had seen the seamless actions between the angels and Amelia in previous ceremonies and she wanted to build that relationship for her daughter's future.

Once the angels arrived, Grace led the ceremony by saying goodbye to the last season.

> *Farewell our Sun,*
> *to your returning light.*
> *I call our honored Goddess,*
> *come through me tonight.*

A porcupine wandered into the Circle; its presence representing a need for caution. Although her eyes remained closed, Grace was very aware of the new presence and so were Amelia and the rest of The Coven.

> *I stir gentle Guardians of the Watchtower,*
> *come all.*
> *Dear Gentle Ancestors,*
> *might you guide us all.*

A white cat walked into the Circle, representing independence and then a lizard followed, bringing wisdom to the ceremony. Grace fell into a trance and let go of the hands she held as she continued. The entire Coven followed with her in mind and in spirit.

> *Tonight with our joining,*
> *the gates of death bring new life.*

And our steps of new balance,
move us away from old strife.
I call you Goddess Isis,
please join us tonight.
In our ceremony of re-birth,
on our world's precious night.

As Grace continued to guide The Coven deeper into the soul of the ceremony, a mischievous fairy appeared on Amelia's shoulder. She tried to ignore him as the soft Winds of the North began to blow, but he was rather persistent and wanted to play.

He tied her hair in knots and began pulling on her ear. Amelia finally peeked one eye open, for just a moment, to confirm it was exactly who she thought it was—Jack, a big troublemaker. Amelia found him amusing but, more often than not, when Jack was around, Amelia also found herself in some sort of trouble. Her mother had warned her about the fairies and what tricksters they can be, but like most children, Amelia could not resist the fun and adventures the enchanted creatures always promised.

Jack was such a distraction that, even though her eyes had just been open, Amelia hadn't seen the group of men sneaking up on The Coven from various points in the park, and neither had Jack. She finally nudged him off of her shoulder with her nose and pressed her eyes closed tight.

The fact that she was trying so hard only taunted Jack. He crawled up the side of her face, grabbed ahold of her eyelashes and pulled her eyelids open, just in time for Amelia to see the shadows surrounding The Coven. A panic rushed over her.

Jack felt her body tense and he was suddenly aware of the presence. He stood straight up just as all of the candles blew out. Amelia turned to warn her mother, only to see a figure, masked by the dark night, raise a dagger high in the air and plunge it down into her mother's chest.

Jack bolted toward the light that glimmered off the knife and, before anyone knew what was happening, he'd grabbed ahold of the attacker by extending his long claws and digging them into his back. He was unable to stop him, but Jack did manage to rip a large piece of flesh from the culprit's right shoulder blade before the attacker and his cohorts disappeared into the night.

Jack turned to Amelia, with his hand full of bloody flesh, only to see the girl's eyes widen as her mother's body fell to the ground.

She didn't scream. She didn't make a sound. She didn't even move. Amelia appeared to be in shock, and perhaps she was, but that did not stop the little girl from what she did next. Amelia closed her eyes in extreme focus and let the ancient soul within her take over. Then the young Witch began to break virtually every law of Wicca and The Craft in a cry for help from the universe.

"I summon the Elements of Air, Fire, Water and Earth …" The Coven members began to open their eyes, realizing that something had gone wrong. They were all horrified and confused to see Grace's body crumbled before them. They rushed to her, wondering how this could have happened, how anyone could have even approached the Circle without them sensing it. Grace's best friend, Summer, immediately took her in her arms and, as The Coven tried to calm themselves, one of the women realized that Amelia was beginning a very serious chant—one too dangerous for even the most practiced of Witches. A look of terror and disbelief came over her.

"Amelia no!" she screamed, alerting The Coven of what the girl was doing.

> … *From the love in my heart and the ache in my soul,*
>   *I summon!*
> *I summon the Winds of the North, the South, the East*
>   *and the West.*
> *I summon all Dragons,*
> *all Fairies,*
> *all Ancestors and Angels,*
> *and the Guardians of the Watchtower*
> *to intervene in harms way …*

"Your mother doesn't want this Amelia!" Summer shouted, but Amelia wasn't paying attention. She was so focused that no one was certain she could even hear Summer.

Amelia continued in a growing and frantic rage.

... To save my mother!
To stop this day!
I SUMMON YOU ALL!
TO STOP THIS DAY!

Amelia repeated her demands over and over again. She summoned every entity she could think of in a chant, unrehearsed, and amazingly powerful. A chant from the pure love in her heart and the fear in her soul that demanded the immediate assistance of those who only come by gentle request when an elder member of a Coven is truly in need.

Because the child's actions were so unworldly, rather than turning to Grace, their leader, who lay on her deathbed, the eyes of The Coven were all on Amelia. She ended her chant and stood still ... waiting. A calm settled in the air, and all was quiet. Then, in a burst of fury and power, they all arrived. First came a tornado of winds, then lightening, thunder and fire, accompanied by the pounding sounds of the Gods rushing to Amelia's aide. Most of The Coven had a hard time keeping their balance in all the chaos, but they could not take their eyes off of the girl. A mortal act, so seemingly irresponsible and undisciplined, was fueled by a power that had never been witnessed. It was not only her force ... what was so amazing about her actions, what would become legendary, was that all who she summoned came. When the winds, the rain and fires calmed, The Coven found itself surrounded by hundreds of angels, deities, ancestors, fairies, salamanders, birds, deer, elk, moose, cats, butterflies, rabbits and bears. It was a moment not of this world, filling all of The Coven with fear and awe. All of The Coven except Amelia, who was concerned only with the well-being of her mother. She stood before Grace, an angel herself, now with broken wings and a blackened heart, as she watched her mother gasp for her final breaths of air. Amelia knelt down to hug her and placed her little hands on Grace's cheeks. Looking into her eyes, she whispered, "Mommy, please don't go. It's not time yet."

Grace wanted nothing more than to hang on for her daughter, but she knew that it was, in fact, time. For whatever reason, Grace's purpose in this life was over and it would be up to Amelia to find her way without her. Grace looked to her daughter with calm eyes, hoping to give Amelia a final memory filled with love; an expression of hope and peace that she would never forget. Amelia stared back at her mother. She saw that Grace was prepared to let go and the fear of losing her took over. She was no longer a strong young Witch, but a scared little girl. "I told you Mommy, it's not time yet. It's not time for you to go."

Grace let her tears flow as she nodded her head. "But it is time, sweetie, and it's okay."

Grace's heart ached as Amelia began to sob. Amelia understood the Pagan reality of existence. She knew of the cycles of life and reincarnation, but these were not her concern. Her only concern at that moment was having a mommy, and although she'd used every bit of strength in her to call on the power of the universe for help, Amelia had failed to keep her mother alive. "But Mommy, how do you know it's time? It might be a mistake. Someone will fix it. They're coming. Just wait."

Grace wrapped her hand around her daughter's and smiled. "Never forget how special you are." The look on Grace's face as she gazed into Amelia's eyes was a look that would not be forgotten. It was a look that would stay with the child for the rest of her life. Amelia's heart fell into her stomach and her hands began to tremble, as a strong and pure fear rushed through her body. She screamed as she watched her mother cough up a mouthful of blood.

"No Mommy! Please. We can make it better," she shouted in a panic as she tried to wipe the blood away with her dress. She looked to The Coven, hysterical. "Please somebody! Please help make her better." Not one of them moved. She turned back to her mother. "You have to stop bleeding!" she screamed, while trying to stop the deluge of blood with her hands.

With Summer's help, Grace again reached for Amelia. She guided her little hand to her mouth and Grace gave Amelia a kiss goodbye. Then Summer tucked Amelia in, closer to her mother, so she could wrap her arms around her. Grace held her daughter as tight as she could. Amelia shook with pain, drenched in her own tears and Grace's blood, as she watched her mommy take her last breath of life; as she watched the woman who created her leave her, all alone in the world. Then she felt the tight grip of her mother's arms lessen until it was gone.

The Coven stood at a distance, unsure of what to do or how to feel. It was an unthinkable tragedy at a time of celebration, of moving from summer to winter and from one cycle to the next, while rejoicing for both the past and the future with the God and Goddess who provide for them. It was a time for balance in the world. The need for balance, they thought, was why Grace was bleeding to death, with no hope to be saved ... and that same need for symmetry was why, one day, Amelia would face what she'd done by the Law of Three. All of the unstabilized energy she'd put out into the world would come back to work against her, at three times the power she'd sent out—not as a punishment for her actions, but because that is simply the way of the Witches. Amelia had created an uncontrolled and chaotic situation that endangered everyone and everything in it by her summons. Some day she would face that same kind of danger, chaos and lack of control, times three. The only questions were—when and how?

Amelia's hands and legs continued to tremble but, with an utterly calm demeanor and focused frame of mind, she got up and turned toward The Coven; the group of supposedly dedicated friends who had done absolutely nothing to help save her mother's life. No one made even the slightest move to go near her. Amelia stood alone in her blood-stained dress, before her mother's corpse, until finally someone had the courage and the heart to take her hand. A feeling of comfort washed over Amelia when she turned to find the little boy beside her, the only other child in The Coven. The warmth of his hand, as he squeezed hers, calmed her. She was strengthened by the fact that he was just as scared, if not more, than she was. The only difference was that he was not afraid to let it show. And, even filled with fear, this young boy, whose family had just moved to California and was brand new to The Coven, was the only person willing to stand by her in the aftermath. He was only person who was struck so profoundly by the idea of growing up without a mother—an event, it appeared, that only the innocence of another child could truly comprehend.

Amelia turned back to Grace and she could see that her mother's soul had already left her body. She was gone and there was no turning back. No way to undo what had been done. *No Goddess, or God or All, who takes a mommy away is good. I won't believe anymore. I DON'T!* Amelia looked back to The Coven, at their fear, at their judgment of her actions. Then she ripped off her ceremonial copper necklace, threw it at them, and ran off into the night.

By running, Amelia broke yet another rule that would come back and work against her, times the Power of Three. By leaving The Coven before the Circle was properly closed Amelia prevented them from closing it completely. She'd let all the energy that had been summoned into the Circle out into the world, unguided and uncontrolled.

Not one member of The Coven moved to go after her, but the young boy could not take his eyes off of Amelia. *Why won't anyone save her? Why won't anyone hug her tight and dry her eyes and tell her everything is going to be okay? What did she do wrong? Why isn't my mommy going to get her? And where is she going?* He wondered, as Amelia ran off blindly into the park and disappeared into the night.

chapter 2

San Francisco, California, September 22, 1984 — Mabon
Earlier That Day

Amelia and her mother sat under the shade of a willowy tree in Golden Gate Park's Japanese Tea Gardens. They had a picnic spread out along with all the makings of a lovely and relaxing afternoon in the park. They were picturesque Celts with jet-black hair and snow-white skin, framed beautifully by the vibrant greens and pink flowers that filled the gardens. The afternoon sun warmed them from the cool bay breeze that swirled through the city. Grace had always enjoyed the park and, ever since Amelia was a baby, it was a place that calmed her like no other. Even as a small child, the Gardens seemed to be an extension of who Amelia was and, it was also only a short walk from their home, so it had become part of their daily afternoon routine.

Amelia braided her mother's long black hair as Grace sipped a steaming cup of boldo tea and read to her daughter from an old tattered storybook titled *The Legend of The One*.

"… That Witch would be as pure as the twins with their strength combined. And on her twenty-eighth birthday, when the moon came closest to the earth, she would be infused with 'The Ultimate Power,' strong enough to overcome her distant Wiccan relative, The Organization, and any other opposition that faced her or what she stood for. Her coming would become legendary in anticipation and throughout history she would come to be known as 'The One.' The End."

"And then what, Mommy?" Amelia knew the story by heart, but she always asked the same questions, as if she was hearing the tale for the very first time.

"That's it."

"But did she come?"

"Not yet."

Amelia wrapped her arms around her mother's neck and looked into her eyes. "But is she coming?" she asked with great concern.

"Nobody knows."

"Why not?"

Grace got up and began packing their things. "Because she hasn't come yet."

"But she is coming, right, Mommy?" she asked, wanting, needing, confirmation that this "One" would someday come and save the world.

"That's what the legend says."

Amelia looked around the park very carefully, spooked and intrigued by the story. Wondering if it was real … and wondering if they were, in fact, alone in the park. "So then the bad Witch baby from the High Priest is coming too? Because there's one good baby and one bad one?"

"That's right."

Amelia pulled on her mother's arm until Grace finally leaned down close to her so Amelia could whisper in her ear, "But where do you think they are right now?"

Grace cupped her hand and leaned in closely to whisper in Amelia's ear, then she shouted, "BOO!" scaring the living daylights out of Amelia, who let out a shriek that turned into a fit of giggles.

"You scared me!"

"I know it. Wasn't that fun?!"

"Yes, but don't do it again, okay?"

"Okay," Grace said looking up to the sky. It was only about an hour away from sunset. "We better get going, honey."

Amelia knew they had an important night ahead of them, but she wanted to stay, so she launched into her usual act of negotiating for more time. She pushed back the thick locks of jet black curls that she always let fall over her face, then she looked up at her mother with her bright, emerald green eyes and, in her most melodramatic voice, she said, "Oh Mommy, why would you want to leave such a beautiful place on such a perfect day? I don't know why we just can't live here."

Grace laughed at her little actress. She'd never been able to resist her daughter's smiling eyes, peeking out through the mop of long curly hair, which she refused to brush. "Oh, okay, miss. You have another half-hour, but you'll recite your homework while we walk."

"Okay," she said.

"When was the Council of America Witches formed?"

"1974."

"What are the thirteen goals of the Witch, as presented by Scott Cunningham?"

Amelia recited as they walked along the garden path. "Know yourself. Know your craft. Learn. Apply knowledge with wisdom." Amelia stopped walking. She couldn't remember what was next. "Blah, blah, blah," she giggled.

"Not blah, blah, blah. What's next?"

Amelia looked to her mother. Grace smiled and raised one foot, balancing on the other, while holding her arms out. "What am I doing?"

That was the clue Amelia needed to continue, "Achieve balance. Keep your words in good order. Keep your thoughts in good order. Celebrate life." Amelia stopped to pick up a rock; then she climbed to the top of a bridge overlooking one of the Gardens' many koi ponds. "Attune with the cycle of life. Breathe and eat correctly. Exercise the body. Meditate ..." Amelia stopped, distracted by the fish.

"And?" Grace said.

"And honor the God and Goddess, Mommy," Amelia said, still entranced by the fish.

"And?" Grace said again.

With a sigh and a big smile Amelia turned to her mother. "And don't forget that people of weakness prey on those who act on negative and reactionary thoughts. We must always be aware of ourselves and our situation. We must do our best to resolve our own negative feelings for the protection of ourselves and of others. We must never use the power of the universe for personal or selfish gain. We must only promote balance in the world and let fate fall where it may. We must not allow ourselves to be tempted into changing what is meant to be, for if we do, we are susceptible to the desires of those who work against us, times three."

Amelia took a deep breath. *That was a mouthful.* It was something that she had taken a great deal of time to memorize, although her mother knew she had not yet begun to understand.

"Very good, honey," Grace climbed down from the bridge. Amelia stayed put. She examined the rock that she'd picked up— its unique shape, the smooth edges, the light shimmer of red that covered it. She held it high above her head, then let it fall into the pond. Her eyes focused on the splash and the ripples in the water created by the disturbance. She was drawn into the spot where the rock hit, as the shape of a pentagram appeared in the water and the ripples multiplied. Amelia recognized the five-pointed star of the Witch immediately and watched, curiously, as it turned clockwise in the water, meaning that it was invoking, bringing positive energy into something or someone. *But for what?* she wondered. *What could be set in motion by a rock just being dropped in the water? Was it the rock? Was it because this was the day of Mabon (MA-bon)?* She didn't know, but the question she did not ask herself was, *Is this because I, Amelia Pivens, dropped the rock?* And the answer to that question was, "Yes." It was because she dropped the rock and the entity that the spinning pentagram was invoking, was her.

Amelia sang her favorite nursery rhyme as she watched the ripples continue to spread out across the water and the pentagram spin.

The itsy bitsy spider
crawled up the water spout.
Down came the rain and
washed the spider out.
Up came the sun and
dried up all the rain.
And the itsy bitsy spider
crawled up the spout again.

A chill suddenly came over her. She felt as though she were being watched. That something, or someone, hurtful was nearby. She scanned the gardens and saw nothing, but there was someone there, far off in the trees, watching every move she made. Diligently waiting for her.

Grace looked up to the setting sun. "Come on Amelia. We've got a lot to do."

As Amelia climbed down the bridge, she took one last look out into the park, but still saw nothing. She turned to her mother, who seemed perfectly content. Amelia knew how intuitive her mother was. She knew that if there were something dangerous nearby, Grace would have sensed it and Amelia could always tell when her mother sensed something.

"Amelia!"

"Yes, Mommy," she shouted as she ran to catch up with her. "I'm here."

As they left the park, the unseen watcher in the distance lingered near them, repeating Amelia's rhyme with unsavory purpose and intent, "The itsy bitsy spider, crawled up the water spout. Down came the rain and washed the spider out ... All in good time, little one ... all in good time."

* * *

Not more than an hour later, Amelia sat at home in a bathtub full of herbs and milk. She drew a pentagram in the water with her finger, remembering how pretty the one in the park was as it spun over the koi in the pond. She wondered if it was still spinning and, if it were, what exactly caused it and what it was invok-

ing. She tried to let go of the thought and clear her head. Amelia
knew that the steamy water was meant to cleanse her body and
mind before the evening ritual and celebration of Mabon, and she
needed to focus on that.

She loved the ritual bath: the smell of the lavender, chamo-
mile and rose oil brought out by the steam; the tingle on her skin
from the peppermint; the soothing comfort of the milk. She could
think of no better way to prepare for the last of the year's eight
sabbats and she could think of no better way to get cleaned up.
She was, after all, seven-years-old and, like most seven-year-old
children, Amelia was not terribly fond of baths.

Mabon is the Pagan and Wiccan celebration of the year's end
and the Autumn Equinox. It falls between September 21st and 23rd,
just one month before the New Year's celebration of Samhain. Amelia
would be attending the Mabon ceremony with her mother. Young
children were not typically included in midnight celebrations, but
Amelia was a powerful child. She was powerful in a way that she
was somewhat aware of, but in no way understood. There is that
which comes naturally in Witchcraft and that which is learned.
Because so much of what Amelia had came naturally, Grace decided, early in her life, that it would be best to let her take part in
the practice at a young age. That way, when she came fully into
her own, it would feel natural and comfortable. The Coven members agreed and, rather than waiting until her teen years, invited
Amelia, when she was still very young, into The Coven.

Grace opened the door to the bathroom, but said nothing,
hoping that Amelia was deep in her meditation. Grace wore a
white linen dress and let her hair cascade down over her shoulders, making it look black as night against the white cloth. She
sprinkled sea salt in the water around Amelia, then watched as her
daughter slid down into the tub to focus and concentrate on the
night festival to come.

Grace went to the counter, untied the silk rope on a small
black velvet bag and took out a necklace. She watched her reflection in the mirror as she fastened the unique, copper pentagram,
donned with jewels representing the element for which each point

of the star stands: white for spirit, blue for water, red for fire, green for earth, and yellow for air. She had made the necklace herself when she became the High Priestess in her Coven. Many Witches wore magickal jewelry, but Grace's choice of copper was unusual. Silver represents the Lady and gold represents the Lord. These metals are often combined to represent the male and the female as one. Grace chose copper, not only because she felt it was the most beautiful, but because it represented The All and for Grace that, in essence, was what Wicca and The Craft were all about.

After locking the clasp on her necklace, Grace turned to her daughter, feeling the weight of the child's stare. Amelia had the eyes of an all-knowing being that stood out against the frame of her tiny body. After a long moment of silence, and Amelia watching her mother very carefully and innocently, she shifted her gaze to the necklace and asked, "Is that where you hide it, Mommy?"

Grace placed her hand over the necklace, forcing Amelia to look back up at her face. "It's not hidden, Amelia. The power is tucked deep in the heart and the soul of every person. We all have it to some degree—every living thing." Grace paused for a moment, waiting for Amelia to say something. She didn't. She simply watched her mother, waiting for her to continue.

"To access your power," Grace said. "You need only to realize that you have it, then allow your mind to let it out. It will happen for you when the time is right. Just remember, you must never fear it or doubt it. You only need acknowledge and embrace what already lives within you for it to shine when your time comes."

"But it only works when you wear your necklace."

"No. The copper is a magickal tool—a symbol I charge with my energy that makes it mine, and mine only. I wear it when I will be leading The Coven or when I want to be recognized for who I am by other Witches, but it is not my power. It only represents it. The real magick is in here," she said as she placed her hands over her heart.

Amelia tilted her head, pondering; still thinking that her mother's magickal abilities somehow came from within the necklace, rather than from within her.

"Once you come into your own, you will understand, little princess," Grace said, as she placed a small copper necklace on the counter for Amelia. It was a tiny replication of the one she was wearing. Amelia's eyes widened with the honor, but she said nothing. She simply took in the meaning, and the gesture, and was immediately determined to live up to it. It was precisely the reaction Grace had expected.

"You know what to do," she said, so proud of her extraordinary daughter. Amelia nodded, very matter-of-factly, then closed her eyes and slipped back down into the water.

William opened the door to the bathroom slowly, trying to be quiet. Dressed in street clothes and covered in sweat and paint, he was clearly no Witch, at least not one taking part in the night's festivities, but it was clear that he was a man in love with his family. He wrapped his arms around Grace and they both watched Amelia. She was deep in her meditation. It was a side of his daughter that had always amazed William—fascinated him. There was something about her, from the depths of her soul that was old, almost ancient. You didn't have to be a Witch to see that. It was something that even her school teachers had commented on, in one way or another. Without taking his eyes off of her, William whispered in his wife's ear, "Is she okay?"

"She's amazing," Grace answered with pride and awe, "and she's going to be like no other."

chapter 3

As soon as the San Francisco authorities released Grace's body, Amelia's father packed only what was absolutely necessary and returned with Amelia, and the remains of his wife, to his family in London. The murder of Grace Pivens went unsolved and Amelia never received an explanation or even a theory from The Coven; something she felt that she more than deserved, something that made her hate Wicca and The Craft even more than before, for robbing her of a mother and her father of the only woman he ever loved.

When he was 18, William Pivens had left his home in England for a, "Summer of Love" experience in California. He met Grace at a park in the Haight-Asbury district on the day he arrived. There was an instant connection and within months they were married.

Grace was a Witch when they met. William knew nothing of The Craft outside the lore he'd heard growing up in a country so riddled with it. It was through Grace that he experienced the true practice. He came to find the concept of Wicca harmonious and beautiful and he eventually honored it as his religious preference. Although a follower of the beliefs, William did not participate in the magickal ceremonies. He was not a Witch, nor did he pretend to be. William understood that practicing Wicca was a choice, but that a true Witch of magick is created at birth and that a practiced man of magick is merely a sorcerer at best. William also knew that, just as his wife was born a Witch, he was born a man of finance with a talent for woodwork. He managed the business of Grace's craft-related writings, jewelry, incense and oils. He also ran his own, making furniture, to the extent that they lived rather comfortably.

The day Grace gave birth to Amelia was truly the happiest day of their marriage and a blessed day for The Coven. Amelia was a born Witch and a pure soul, just like her mother. From the day she could walk, Amelia practiced Witchcraft and Wicca. She studied with her mother and attended all of the workshops and ceremonies, until the night of her mother's murder. After that, she turned her back on The Craft and everything it stood for, and never looked back. William had made that easy with a move to another country and a complete lifestyle change.

Amelia was raised a proper British girl by her father and her grandparents. It was a strict and structured life. It was everything that San Francisco wasn't and that's what Amelia loved most. The practice of Witchcraft was never discussed or even acknowledged as part of their past. William wouldn't stand for it. Not after he'd opened their front door, at two o'clock in the morning, to his daughter's pounding fists to find her alone and drenched in her mother's blood.

Amelia's grandfather, a rather significant and well-to-do banker, was happy to properly spoil his only grandchild. And her grandmother, a prominent woman of society, did enjoy showing her off as she was so amazingly beautiful and smart, even as a young child. Amelia never wanted for anything, yet never asked for much either. She was a private and quiet girl, deeply affected by the loss of her mother and happy to be so far away from the world in which they had once lived. She spent most of her childhood quietly drawing or painting in her grandfather's massive study. She loved being surrounded by the old dark woods, the smell of the furniture that her grandfather took such good care of and the many books that lined the walls. She'd made an agreement with herself that she would read each and every one of those books before the end of her life. She was sure that when she was done she would have the answer to every question ever asked, maybe even why her mother was taken away from her when she was only seven-years-old.

Amelia studied at the finest schools, eventually majoring in fine art and anthropology and securing a coveted position at The National Gallery, London, after the publication of her in-depth writing on the Spanish painter, Francisco Goya. Of course, it didn't hurt that the museum's curator was Jeremy Roth, an old family friend, but there was never any accusation, inside or outside the world of art, that Amelia had not earned the position on her own merit. After her writings were published, her insight led many to believe that she was a distant relative to Goya, or had somehow been exposed to information—journals it was suspected—that no critic or historian had seen before. However, that was not at all true; it was only well thought-out speculation. Amelia had always approached the man and his art as though she knew him on the most intimate level. She had reacted in this manner ever since she first saw his work and it was her emotional reaction, or "connection" to him that she frequently spoke of in her papers, making her approach, in actuality, more philosophical than historical. It was this unconventional approach that made her papers so interesting.

It was shortly after she and her father had arrived in London that Amelia saw Francisco Goya's work for the first time. Jeremy was giving them a private tour of The National Gallery and Amelia wandered off. She'd been drawn to the corner of a small room in the East Wing. Jeremy and William found her sitting quietly in front of "The Forcibly Bewitched," contemplating its true meaning and Goya's motivation. Both men were curious and taken back by her serious disposition when they found her. After a moment of hesitation, Jeremy asked, "What do you see, Amelia?"

Without taking her eyes off of the painting, she answered, "A man who is scared."

"And why is he scared?"

"Because he doesn't understand," she said with a full comprehension of precisely what she was saying. "He's scared so much that his stomach hurts, but he also wants to know."

"What does he want to know?"

Amelia turned to Jeremy with a serious expression and a furrowed brow. "He wants to know the truth. He's scared because he wants to know the real truth, instead of all the stories his mommy made up when he was little ... She should have just told him."

William and Jeremy were stunned. They looked to each other, but were at a loss for words to comment. This was a child who had just turned eight.

"Little Amelia Pivens," Jeremy said. "I can't tell you how much I'd like to climb inside that head of yours so that I could see the clock that makes it tick."

"There's not a clock in my head, Mr. Roth," she said and she turned back to the painting, again lost in its story within an instant.

Amelia's interest in Goya began, then and there, and it was a fascination from which she was never to stray far. William eventually came to the conclusion that her fascination sprang from the fact that Amelia's first exposure to Goya came through one of his Witchcraft-inspired paintings and perhaps his little girl was looking for the answers to her mother's death in the painter's work. In any case, both William and Jeremy knew that Amelia was special in a way that they did not yet understand. When she was only eight, she peered at life through the other side of the looking glass in a manner that both fascinated and frightened them.

* * *

Shortly after she began working at The National Gallery, Amelia married one of Europe's youngest and most promising classical pianists, Wolfgang Kreutzer. They had met, by accident, in Paris after one of his concerts. Amelia had not been to see him; rather she was across the street, at a café, to meet a colleague from The Louvre, whom she had only met once before. Wolfgang was German with white blonde hair and bright blue eyes. He looked strikingly similar to the man she was waiting for. Wolfgang noticed her the moment she walked in and, when her eye caught his, she smiled and walked over. He thought she was incredibly beautiful, with her endless smile and sparkling eyes, so when Amelia took a chair, said hello, introduced herself to his friends, then began rambling on about art, he just let her go. It was almost an hour before the man she was intended to meet arrived, terribly apologetic for getting caught up at the museum.

"Please, you mustn't apologize," Wolfgang said, as Amelia's mistake was revealed. "Join us," he said to the man.

Amelia blushed from head to toe as her colleague pulled up a chair, rather amused as he realized what had happened. She could feel the redness coming over her face and chest and she knew she could do nothing to hide it. What she didn't see, at the time, was that her reaction only deepened Wolfgang's attraction to her. "My name is Wolfgang Kreutzer," he finally said with a smile. She shook his hand and after a moment his name registered in her head. Amelia's jaw dropped, as did that of her colleague.

"Wolfgang Kreutzer?" she repeated, as she turned and looked out the window to the concert hall across the street. His name covered a large marquee, advertising that he'd played a sold-out concert earlier that evening. Wolfgang Kreutzer was a world-renowned classical pianist and Amelia was mortified. Wolfgang smiled and raised his glass to Amelia's colleague, "To being late ..." then he looked to Amelia, "... and to mistaken identities."

"Salude!" the table roared as they all raised their glasses and drank in celebration of what was clearly a case of true love at first sight.

Amelia and Wolfgang were married less then a year later and the couple lived what could only be called a charmed life. After three years of marriage, they still appeared as newlyweds on their honeymoon. Amelia spent her days at the Gallery and her nights at Wolfgang's concerts. When he traveled, so did she, guest lecturing at various museums on behalf of The National Gallery, with their blessings. Amelia's family couldn't have been happier. Wolfgang was the only person who had truly touched her since the death of her mother and the smile that he brought to her face, her grandmother always said, was the Pivens family's greatest treasure.

* * *

On the night before Amelia's twenty-fifth birthday, Wolfgang played at one of London's oldest and most beautiful concert halls. Amelia sat in the front row with her father, her boss, Jeremy Roth, and a few close friends. Her father had come to watch Amelia almost as much as he'd come to see Wolfgang's concert. She would become so entranced by the music and her love for her husband, when he played, that William could see and almost touch his daughter's fairy tale romance—the romance that she so deserved. It was a romance for which William would have traded his own life, if he'd only known what that night would bring.

Wolfgang played Amelia's favorite piece to conclude the evening, Ludwig Von Beethoven's *Symphony No. 6 in F major*, op.68 "Pastoral." Although there was not one empty seat in the house, it was as though Wolfgang was playing only for Amelia, as though they were the only two people in the room. The depth and passion of the piece took Wolfgang out of this world, and his willingness to go there was what always took the audience along with him. He closed the evening and left the crowd in awe and wanting more.

The spirit of the music continued to fill them, even as Amelia and Wolfgang left the concert hall and stepped out on to the busy city sidewalk. Amidst a number of concert guests, they walked to the corner and waited for the light to change. It was then Amelia spotted their friends across the street. They were all wearing party hats.

"There they are," she waved. "What have they got on?" A clock tower struck midnight and Wolfgang smiled at her. He had a surprise.

"Well, it is now officially your birthday." The traffic light changed and, along with a mob of pedestrians, they began to cross the street.

"What have you done?"

"Everything … This is only the beginning."

Amelia shrieked and giggled with excitement. Then, suddenly, a black town car rounded the corner, skidding out of control. It barreled through the crowd. People were screaming, pushing and pulling in every direction. A man pulled Amelia out of the way and they watched as the town car sped off into the night.

Many people were hurt, but it was all minor. Blood was dripping from a gash in Amelia's head as she stood up and scanned the area for Wolfgang. The screams and cries of her friends and onlookers filled the air as they hurried over to help.

Amelia didn't see her husband anywhere. "Wolfgang!" she shouted, beginning to panic, so much so that all the noises around her became slowed and muffled and all that she could hear was her own heart beating. She finally saw him, lying in the street, badly injured.

"Oh, God," she cried, and ran to him. He was covered in blood and his legs were crushed. She looked into his eyes, relieved to find him conscious. He was breathing, but struggling. "You're going to be okay."

Wolfgang shook his head and reached for her. Amelia took his hands in hers, thinking that he was worried about his fingers, that he would never play again. "You're going to be fine," she assured him, looking only at his hands, not realizing that the real damage was in his chest. The car had crushed his torso; all his ribs were broken and the internal bleeding was unstoppable. He knew. He knew and he could feel his body dying. Amelia ran her hands through his hair. She wanted to relax him, to soothe him as much as she could until the paramedics arrived. "You're okay."

Wolfgang closed his eyes to take a breath and forced a smile as he looked to his precious wife, knowing full-well that he was not going to be okay. He tried to take her hand back in his. He wanted to tell her something, but he was struggling. She put her hand in his and moved in close until their cheeks were touching. "What is it?" her voice trembled.

With all of his strength, he brought her hand to his mouth and kissed it. Then, in not more than a whisper, Wolfgang managed the words, "I love you."

The color drained from Amelia's face as she pulled back to see the look in his eyes—as she realized she was watching her husband take his last breath of life. He was gone. Just like that. She

wanted to say something, but she didn't know what. She wanted
to scream, but when she opened her mouth only a muted squeal
came out of her. The blood rushed through her body, her adrenaline kicked in and, if she'd had the means, Amelia would have
taken her own life right then and there. In that moment, she was
desperate to die, horrified to find herself breathing, and when she
finally cried out it seemed the whole city of London shook with
her pain, only to be followed by the echoing sobs of her shattered
heart and her, once again, broken soul.

PART TWO

chapter 4

London England, October 17
Two Years and Eleven Months Later

Amelia Pivens Kreutzer was a stunning woman who, at the age of only twenty-seven, had seen a lifetime of hurt. Her losses showed in her deep green eyes, which she hid behind her mop of long black hair, the same way she did as a child. She stood, looking out her father's bedroom window, at the rainy London afternoon. The street outside the Pivens family Eaton Square residence was dark and quiet. Amelia rolled the wedding band, which hung on a chain around her neck, through her delicate fingers, knowing she should remove it, but unwilling to take it off completely. Amelia had turned the ring into a necklace.

She still talked to Wolfgang. She thought of him every day. It was his memory that kept her going most of the time, but that also filled her with a relentless sorrow. She withdrew when he died just as she had when she lost her mother, but with Wolfgang's death it was clear that Amelia probably would not recover. All she could do was throw herself into her work and, with the encouragement of her father and the staff at The National Gallery, whom she had come to consider family, that's exactly what she did.

Amelia worked so hard that she was asked to take paid days, even weeks, off. She never made the effort for personal advancement but, nonetheless, she soon found herself with the title of "Associate Director," working right beside long-time family friend and Director/Curator of The National Gallery, Jeremy Roth. He watched her bring life to the museum through a dedication driven by the death in her own life. He only hoped that one day he would see her smile again—that same smile which her mother could never say "no" to and which Wolfgang loved her for—but it didn't seem as though that time would come soon, if ever.

On that cold day, Amelia had called in, not because she finally wanted to take a day trip or a long weekend, or even just to take a walk through the streets of the city. She'd called in because her father was sick and he wanted her to come over for a talk. And there they were, Amelia at the window and William in bed. They were only a few feet away from each other, with so much to say, in a completely silent room.

William was feeling better, but he was still bedridden. He had been for several months. His eyes were set on an old photograph of Grace, Amelia and himself. As he stared at it all of the old feelings came back to him. He had never known so much love. *What a family*, he thought. *No one could have asked for much more. How could I have let this happen? What could I have done to protect my wife? To keep my daughter from such a horrifying experience? Why couldn't I have raised her as a happy, normal girl? And what, in God's name, am I supposed to do with this secret?* It was a secret that he'd buried deep inside him; one that he'd gone through so much hell to keep. What would Amelia think of the truth? Was it possible she could feel any more pain in her life, or had she come to expect it? If he told her, would she withdraw even more? Or would she just become numb? *More numb, if that was even possible.* He didn't know and he wanted nothing more than to let his secret die with him, but he knew that wasn't an option. He had to tell her. He had to tell Amelia everything.

William watched his daughter. How she held her wedding band and stared out the window as though she were looking for Wolfgang, as though he might somehow walk up the front steps and knock on the door.

"Your birthday is coming," William finally said.

Amelia's gaze remained fixed on the view beyond the window. She watched carefully as a black town car pulled up and parked just across the street. "It's a whole month away Daddy … and I'm still not ready to celebrate."

"I know," William said, understandingly. He knew, after what happened to her husband on her birthday three years earlier, that his sweet child would probably never celebrate her birthday again. But that was not why he'd asked Amelia over and he knew that if he did not get to the point now, he might never. His hands shook when he finally managed to say, "I did everything that I could to keep you away from The Craft … and The Craft away from you." Amelia turned around, shocked and completely taken off guard by her father's words. Then she saw his shaky hands holding the photograph of the two of them with Grace. He quickly set it down on the bed next to him. Amelia considered the look in her father's eyes. *His meds are kicking in,* she told herself, blaming the drugs for his comment.

She sat down on the bed next to him, telling herself that he might be over medicated or suffering a fever—hoping that was the case. *What else would make him say such a thing after so many years? Witches were not spoken of in the Pivens family, not even on Halloween. Not for twenty years. Not ever.*

"Please know that I tried," he said, ashamed to look in her eyes, but unable to turn away.

The sight of his emotional struggle left a sickening feeling in Amelia's stomach. "Yes. Yes, you did. And it worked. Daddy we don't talk about The Craft. Why …"

"Because I had always hoped it would work," he said, cutting her off, desperate to finish what he had to say while he had the strength to do it. "I thought if I believed enough, I could change it."

"Change what?"

"Fate, Amelia … I'm sorry. I was wrong. Your mother was right. I should have paid more attention."

"Paid more attention to what? What were you wrong about Daddy?"

"I didn't know how to tell you and quite frankly, I never wanted to. I was never convinced that the legend was true." William brushed Amelia's hair from her eyes and placed his hands over hers. "Until now."

Amelia wanted nothing more than to get up and call the nurse, but she knew that turning away from her father in that moment would hurt him deeply.

"I thought that by moving back to London, with my family, and by ignoring all of your mother's old acquaintances and everything that had to do with them, it would all just go away. All I ever wanted was for you to be happy. What you saw. What you experienced. It was all too much. It was too much for anyone and you were just a little girl. I moved us here because I wanted you to be free."

"I am free," she said with great confidence, resisting the doubt that was growing in the pit of her stomach. From a door in her mind, that she'd closed and forgotten long ago, seeped a knowing that her father might be speaking from a position of sound mind and clarity. If that was the case, Amelia did not want to hear what he had to say. She told herself that his words were a result of his illness and age, not because she believed it, but because it was what she needed to believe ... because that was all that she could handle.

The thoughts racing through her mind did not go unnoticed by her father. It was actually the reaction he'd expected and he knew quickly that this was not the right time, that even if she listened, she would not truly hear him because she just didn't want to. Knowing his daughter as well as he did, William had prepared a letter as an alternative. He opened the drawer to his bedside table, removed an envelope and held it out to her.

"What's this?" she asked pointedly, having decided that the conversation her father had summoned her there for was over.

"I'm the last of your family, Amelia, and when I'm gone, things will change quickly and dramatically."

"Daddy."

"I'm serious."

"I know that you believe certain things because you have to, because you loved Mommy so much and she believed, but ..."

She picked up a pill bottle and scanned the label. "How many of these are you taking?" she asked.

"I'm serious, Amelia. I understand this is not the time, so please, just take the letter."

"Pills like this can cause paranoia."

William's voice sharpened and he addressed Amelia as though he were scolding her, which was a rarity, even when she was a child. "I'm not paranoid, Amelia. I'm planning and I need you to do the same."

"The nurse says you've been doing so much better and now what do we have here? Funeral arrangements? Your will? Is that what this is?" she demanded, knowing full well that the contents of the envelope her father was holding out to her was not his will or his funeral arrangements. She left him hanging, holding the letter out to her because she didn't want to touch it. She didn't want it to be real. Amelia knew that it was something to do with her; *something else* that she didn't know and surely didn't want to—something to do with The Craft. She had no interest in the letter whatsoever, but her father's eyes were pleading with her.

Please my darling daughter. Please just take it.

"It's all I can do for you now," he said, extending the letter, struggling to hold it with his weakening hand.

When Amelia saw her father's eyes fill with tears, she took the letter and her voice softened. "I'm sorry, Daddy. I'll read it. I'll read your letter."

"Thank you. It's important."

"I understand. Do you want me to call the nurse?"

"I'm fine," he smiled with relief; disappointed that she didn't want to talk, but satisfied that she'd taken the letter that he believed would save her life.

When the business at hand was completed, William wanted to lighten the mood. Amelia was more than happy to go along with him. Denial had been a popular Pivens family tradition ever since they lost Grace and there was no sense in changing things at this juncture.

"How about some tea?" she asked.

"That sounds lovely."

William's forced smile marginally covered his fear and concern for Amelia. She got up, relieved to be leaving the room for a few minutes.

"I love you Daddy."

"I love you too, sweetheart."

Amelia walked toward the door. "Do you want milk?" she asked as she turned to her father. Their eyes met and Amelia's blood ran cold. It was the look in his eyes—a look that she'd seen twice before, first in her mother and later in her husband. A look that had come to haunt her—and here it was again.

"I love you," he said and without forewarning, William Pivens took his last breath of life right in front of his daughter.

"Daddy!!!"

Amelia's body went numb and she screamed the frightened cry of a lost child—a scream that seemed loud enough to shatter glass. Her eyes swelled with tears and a wretched pain, too unfair for any human to experience, took over her body.

Then, out of nowhere, the sound of a car engine from the street below filled the room, startling Amelia. It was unusually loud, considering she was on the second floor and the windows were all shut tight. She turned and watched as the black town car pulled away from the curb. She looked from the car to her father and back again, as if the driver had stolen her father's soul and was making off with it, right in front of her—the bastard Grim Reaper, finding it necessary to show himself in action once again.

"What do you want?!" she screamed, and the music of Beethoven's "Pastoral" filled her mind as Amelia watched the car drive away. She heard it exactly that way Wolfgang had played it that final night. It pounded through her as she looked back to her father, then down at the sealed envelope that he'd just given her.

"Jesus, God, what is this?" she said to herself, knowing that whatever was in the envelope would explain what had just happened. She began to sob even harder because more than anything in the world, Amelia wanted to ignore it; to burn the letter; never to have known about it. She watched her warm tears slide down her face and hit the paper, one after the other.

All she could think of and all she could hope for was that this wasn't really happening. That she didn't just lose the only family she had left. That this was all a bad dream and she would wake up any minute.

chapter 5

October 20

　　Amelia stood in the funeral home where she'd been, just two years earlier, when her grandparents were killed in a car accident, and the year before that when she buried her husband. It was the same man who greeted her. It was the same man who had greeted her father when Grace's body was flown in from California to rest in the Pivens' Family Plot; the same place where, one day, William would lie next to his wife and finally rest in peace.

　　The man's name was Mr. Paskin. He was an old man with kind eyes and warm hands. She'd forgotten that about him until they shook hands once again. Amelia's hands and feet were icy to the touch. Wolfgang always told her that, "Cold hands mean you have a warm and loving heart." She'd remembered that the day she came to see Mr. Paskin about her husband's service. She'd wondered what it meant when he took her hand in his and felt comfort in the warmth of his grasp. If her cold hands were a result of her warm heart, then who was this man and why did her moments with him seem as if they were his sole concern? How could a man with a heart as icy as her hands put her at ease?

　　The idea overtook her and invited a string of others, in her mind, as she stood with Mr. Paskin once more. *Is this the life of a twenty-seven-year-old woman?* she wondered. *Do other women my age come to know the proprietor of the local funeral home? And what must this man think of me?* It was not that Amelia was feeling sorry for herself, but she couldn't help wonder what exactly fate had in store for her and how her life must look to those whom she'd encountered often, but never really knew.

"Mrs. Kreutzer, are you okay?" Amelia looked up at Mr. Paskin, realizing that, while all these thoughts were running through her head, he'd been talking to her, asking her questions. She hadn't heard him. She hadn't even noticed.

"Mr. Paskin. I'm so sorry. I don't know ... I wasn't here for a moment I guess."

"It happens, luv," he said with a warm and knowing tone. "It's all part of the process and God knows you've been through enough already."

"Yes. Thank you. So, where should we begin? I know I've done this before, but I can't remember exactly what we need to do," she said with truth and a deep realization. She had done this before and more than once, but she couldn't remember the process or really even being there before for that matter, with the exception of Mr. Paskin's handshake.

"Your father left very specific instructions, Amelia. He didn't want you to have to do anything. He'd asked the doctor to call me on his passing and he gave me a list of instructions and payment in full."

Amelia was a little surprised, but her father had always been a planner so it made sense, she guessed.

"Oh ... well. Thank you, Mr. Paskin. I suppose I'll be going then."

"Yes, Madam."

"Please, call me if there's anything."

"I will. The service is set for a week from Saturday."

"That's ten days away. Why not sooner?"

"It was all in your father's instructions, but we can certainly move it up."

"No. That's okay. I'm sure he had his reasons. Thank you."

As Amelia started toward the door, she was hit with a question. "Mr. Paskin, when did my father leave you these instructions?"

"Just a few weeks ago. I can't remember the day ... Oh, yes I can, I remember because it was the Autumn Equinox, the twenty-third of September, I think. A Wednesday. I was reading about it in the paper when he phoned." Amelia didn't say anything, she just took in the information.

My father called to make his funeral arrangements on Mabon? A Wiccan sabbat and the anniversary of her mother's murder. A wave of nausea passed over her. *What was it that he knew?* she wondered.

"Is everything okay?" Mr. Paskin asked with concern.

"Yes. Thank you. Thank you for everything," Amelia said as she hurried out the door. "Have a good evening."

Mr. Paskin's heart went out to Amelia as she walked away, fumbling through her emotional hell, all alone in the world once again.

chapter 6

October 23

A heavy October rain pounded against Amelia's office window as she sipped her morning coffee and did her best to focus on work. After three years of persistence and calling in favors, she had finally put together her dream exhibition. The National Gallery would host the largest-ever exhibit of Francisco Goya's work, including collections from museums world-wide as well as privately owned pieces. Everything was in place, with the exception of *The Prado* in Madrid, whose collection was vast and incredibly important.

The *Prado*'s commitment would determine where, in the museum, Amelia would present the exhibit. She'd requested the entire East Wing, to Jeremy's amusement. The East Wing made up one third of the museum and clearing an entire wing was so massive an idea, he hadn't thought she was serious. Then, when she told him that she intended to borrow *The Black Paintings* collection from *The Prado* and replicate the walls of Goya's home, *Quinta del Sordo*, where they had originally hung, Jeremy agreed, but only if *The Prado* committed in full. While they had agreed verbally, they had failed to sign the contract or begin sending the paintings and Amelia had become more than a little worried. Then the week before William's passing, Jeremy was contacted by *The*

Prado's Curator, Señor Martel Demingo. He said he would come to London and make his final decision about which paintings would be made available when he arrived.

All that Amelia could do was hope and wait. All the other pieces were already in transit and, on Halloween night, the Goya exhibit would open, with or without *The Prado*'s participation.

Claude Benson, The National Gallery's oldest and most trusted guard, as well as Amelia's favorite, knocked on the open door of her office. "Good morning," Amelia said, smiling at the sight of him.

"I'm so sorry."

"Thank you. His service is next Saturday."

"Jeremy told us," Claude looked at her with the concern of a father, noticing the dark circles under her eyes that she'd tried to cover with make-up, her shaky hands and uneasy disposition. "Are you sure you should be …" but he couldn't find the words. His paternal instincts just wanted to hug her and tell her everything was going to be okay and she should go home and rest, but he knew that things would never be okay for little Amelia Pivens. He also knew how much work she had to do and how little time she had to do it in. "Do you think you want a little more time off?" he finally asked.

"I'm not ready. I need to go through, day-to-day—business as usual, for now."

Claude smiled. She'd always been such a focused and determined girl. "Okay, then I have a surprise for you, Madam." Amelia sat straight up with anticipation while Claude knowingly teased her. "It's in from the *Real Academia de Bellas Artes de San Fernando* in Madrid."

She jumped out of her seat. The arrival of a new piece was the only thing that could truly give her a break from her life right now and Amelia knew that just as well as Claude did.

* * *

Amelia and Claude stood in the museum receiving room with two trusted staff members. Although in a somber state, this was Amelia's favorite part of the job; her own little version of Christmas. The tradition had become that, when a painting arrived, Claude and Amelia would watch as it was uncrated. Then Amelia would share the story behind the art with him.

She was exhilarated as the men opened the crate and revealed the painting. "His *Self-Portrait In the Studio*! It's amazing isn't it? This one is my favorite."

"Well then," Claude said, anxious to hear what she had to say. "Please elaborate."

"For Francisco Goya's *Self-Portrait In The Studio* he put himself under his own unforgiving, looking glass. I find this to be the most honest and the most compelling of his self-portraits ... he's so present. Just look at him. It's as if he's stepped into the room with us."

"Is it the honesty in his approach that makes this one your favorite?"

"Yes and no. It's not just his work," she said as she fell under the painter's gaze and her eyes locked with Goya's. "It's him. Strong subject and strong painter combined ... in painting himself, in looking in that mirror armed only with his brushes, Goya was unable to deny who he was. His aggression, his impulses ... the precondition of unstable thoughts and borderline madness necessary to embark on the creative process. He was bold and revealing, feared and fearful, confident and full of doubt. A pure contradiction. He wasn't only a man of pure art. He was a pure man and he was able to know that ... to revel in his work. It's not just the painting, it's the concept. I find the ability to be that honest with yourself, extraordinary."

Amelia snapped out of the trance she'd fallen under and turned to Claude. "I just launched into one of my pretentious lecture voices, didn't I?"

"I rather enjoy your pretentious lecture manner, Madam."

"There's just something about Goya that consumes me, sometimes. Maybe I knew him in a past life."

"Maybe you *were* him in a past life."

"Now there's an interesting thought," said Jeremy Roth. The wealthy and distinguished Englishman was frequently described

as the spitting image of Sir Anthony Hopkins. Jeremy had snuck
in, with another man, to listen as Amelia elaborated on Goya's
Self-Portrait in the Studio. "How are you doing my dear?" he asked,
as he lovingly placed his hand on her shoulder.

Amelia hugged him tight. Her eyes welled with tears. Jeremy
was like family and he was the only person she could let her guard
down in front of. And for some reason, at that moment, she just
couldn't help it. "I'm okay," she said. "It's easier to be here." She
stopped herself; afraid she might break down.

"I know," Jeremy said as Amelia pulled away from him, in the
hopes of looking professional for the man he'd walked in with. He
was a shockingly handsome Spaniard, in his early thirties with
dark hair, hazel eyes and a warm presence.

"I'm very sorry for your loss," the man said.

"Thank you …" she looked to him, having no idea who he was.

"My name is Martel," he said with a soft, alluring smile.

"Martel Demingo from *The Prado*?!" She turned to Jeremy.
"Does this mean?" Jeremy winked at her. *Yes it does.* Amelia jumped
in the air and started clapping her hands. Martel and Jeremy
laughed.

"We are happy to loan all of the Goyas you requested and
reconstruct the setting for *The Black Paintings* here at The National Gallery. We also agree that having the opening night gala
on Halloween is an excellent idea," Martel said, thrilled by and
rather attracted to the excitement that had come over Amelia.

She embraced him like an old friend, without thinking, sur-
prising both of them. These were not the actions of a proper British lady and certainly not of one who had been assigned to The
National Gallery, but Amelia was so excited and relieved that she
just couldn't hold back and Martel thought she was wonderful
because of it.

Jeremy watched her with delight. Her response was even better than he'd hoped for. He waited a moment so that Amelia could
catch her breath and then he told her the rest. "You realize this
means that your request to clear the entire East Wing for the exhibit is granted. You're going to need the space."

She teared up, conflicted by feelings of sorrow for her father and of exhilaration over the accomplishment. "Thank you. I'm sorry. The timing just makes it all a little bittersweet." As she wiped her eyes and took a deep breath Amelia considered all of the work she had ahead of her. Martel watched the look on her face as the tremendous task at hand registered. *It's going to take a miracle*, she thought, but she would pull it off. Moving mountains had become one of her pastimes over the years.

"Mrs. Kreutzer, because of the limitations on time, I've taken the liberty of hiring a private jet and putting on extra staff to get the paintings here quickly and safely."

"Fantastic," she sighed with relief. "I have a construction crew on hold to build the walls replicating *Quinta del Sordo*. Shall we discuss the details over lunch?" She turned to Jeremy. "We need to call the insurance company right away and the alarm installation supervisor, and ..."

The phone rang and Claude picked it up as Amelia continued to rattle off a list of things to do. Jeremy nodded and smiled. He didn't need a list. He was her supervisor after all and he knew what needed to be done, but it was Amelia's process to ramble on when she was excited and it was something about her that Jeremy had always found endearing, so he let her go on.

Claude interrupted, holding out the phone to Amelia. "It's Scotland Yard. A Detective Carlisle." Martel, Jeremy and Amelia all turned to each other. Why on earth would Scotland Yard be calling her? Amelia took the phone from Claude, who directed his worried eyes toward Jeremy. Something had happened. Something unexpected and very wrong had happened and the weight of it filled the room.

chapter 7

Detective Denny Carlisle's deep and steady eyes seemed to penetrate Amelia as he continued his questioning. He had the demeanor of a family man rounding forty, with a lock of red hair that advertised his Irish heritage. He smelled of the same aftershave William had always worn. The familiar scent filled Amelia with sudden memories of lost love and comfort, made all the more disconcerting considering where she was and what she was doing. Scotland Yard was, by all means, a place where one felt the need to focus. She was trying, but not doing so well. The detective addressed her with care and courtesy, but also with reservation. He sensed that there was more to the story than Amelia and Jeremy were letting on. He had just informed them that the body of William Pivens was stolen from the funeral home in broad daylight and their only reaction was silence.

"Did your father have any enemies?" the detective asked for the third time.

"No," Amelia answered with disdain. "You asked me that already."

"I'm sorry, Madam."

"It's alright," she said. The truth was that she had no idea who would steal her father's body, but she suspected she would find out why it was stolen if she read the letter he'd given her. The letter that was still lying on her dining room table unopened. She'd considered not reading it at all, but this situation left her with no choice. She would read it, but she certainly wouldn't tell the detective or Jeremy about it, not yet anyway.

Jeremy noticed that Amelia was beginning to drift from the conversation so he jumped in to help move the process along, "What makes you ask that, Detective? He's already passed."

"And even if he did have an enemy, why would they steal his body?" Amelia added.

The detective was becoming increasingly suspicious of both of them, wondering why they seemed more defensive and agitated than distraught and concerned. "There is no telling what someone with a grudge will do, Madam. Is there any chance that he wanted an unconventional burial, something that might give a friend a reason to take the body? Meaning no harm, of course."

"No. He's to be buried in the family plot. He even had my mother brought from The States so they would be there together one day ... I'm sorry, but shouldn't you be out looking for him?"

"Yes, Madam. There is a whole team already working on it."

"Thank you ... Is there a ladies room I can use?"

"Around the corner and on your right."

Amelia left the room, the two men turned to each other and the tone immediately became much more formal and direct. "You've been a family friend for how long?" the detective asked Jeremy.

"Virtually Amelia's whole life. I knew her mother in The States. Grace died when Amelia was seven. That's when they moved back. I've seen Amelia and William on a regular basis since then."

"Nothing out of the ordinary?"

"No."

"Any strange affairs or women that might want to ..."

"He was a decent man," Jeremy interrupted.

Define decent was the only thought running through the detective's head. He knew exactly who Jeremy Roth was and he also knew that Jeremy and William were both from old British families, with old British money which, in Detective Carlisle's experience, usually meant they also had old and colorful British secrets that they would go to great lengths to keep secret.

"Can we go now?" Amelia asked, letting the men know that she'd returned. They were both too caught up in the battle of personal will they were exercising in their exchange to notice.

"It's just that I'm exhausted," she added, which was obviously true. It was also clear she'd been crying in the bathroom. Her make-up had washed away and the dark circles around her eyes showcased her puffy, red eyelids. Detective Carlisle saw her pain and felt for her, but he could only wonder what this young woman was hiding. Whatever it was, was clearly eating at her from the inside out. And whatever it was, he was determined to find out, although he knew then that any information from Amelia would not come voluntarily. He would have to find it another way.

He gave her a nod, "Ring up, if you think of anything."

"We will," Jeremy answered for both of them in a firm tone, as if to make sure the detective understood that, no matter the circumstances, he would be present in the investigation and if Scotland Yard wanted anything with Amelia, they would also be dealing with him. Then he smiled, "Thank you, Detective Carlisle, for all of your time and concern. I know that you will have this sorted out promptly."

"We'll do our best, Mrs. Kreutzer. Until we find out what's happened here, and why, keep an extra eye out."

"Why?" Amelia asked as she leveled her defensive eyes on the detective with fear and ferocious intensity, wondering just what he thought he knew … and what he actually did know.

"He doesn't mean to frighten you," Jeremy assured her.

"No, but we don't know what motivated this, Madam, and we always suggest that a person exercise caution until we have a handle on the situation."

"You'll stay with me," Jeremy said, for the first time agreeing with the detective, which by no means went unnoticed.

"Very good. Should I need anything, I'll contact you at Mr. Roth's residence."

"Oh … thank you, but I really just want to sleep in my own bed, around my things."

"I understand," Jeremy said, not at all surprised by her refusal.

"I'll update you tomorrow," Detective Carlisle held the door for them.

"Thank you, Detective," Amelia tried to smile, but she couldn't. There was a great deal that had just been left unsaid and all three of them knew it. She had not seen the last of the detective and she knew that too. This was only the beginning, but of what she had no idea.

* * *

Driving home with Jeremy, Amelia was emotional. She felt claustrophobic being strapped in by a seatbelt; trapped in Jeremy's car. *Maybe it's the car,* she thought. Jeremy collected cars and his latest was a gun-metal gray Aston Martin V12 Vanquish. She loved it. She'd teased him by asking to borrow it on more than one occasion, but now the confines of its interior felt small. She may as well have been in the glove box. She wanted out. She rolled down the window, but she couldn't get the sense of the fresh air she so desperately needed. It was as if her lungs were collapsing and her chest was shrinking. She felt as if her head might explode at any moment. She had to get out of the car. Before Jeremy was able to come to a complete stop outside her South Kensington flat, Amelia had the door open and one foot out.

"I'll see you in," he said, noticing she looked as white as a sheet, barring the black and yellow circles that masked her eyes.

"I'm fine. Really." She hugged him. "Thank you. I just ... I'm just going to have some tea and go to bed."

"Are you sure?"

"Yes."

"Alright, but whatever you need, Amelia, I'm here."

"Thank you. I don't know what I would do without you. I just need to be alone right now."

"I understand."

Amelia got out of the car and Jeremy waited while she walked up the stairs and opened the front door. As she walked through the dark front room to turn on a light, the large figure of a man moved, quickly and quietly, toward the front door. Amelia sensed something and turned, but the man was already gone.

Jeremy was still outside in the car. He was about to pull away, when he saw the man disappear down the street, but he hadn't seen exactly where he came from. He was moving too fast and it was too dark for Jeremy to identify him. All that stood out was the shine of light coming from the man's copper ring and that was enough to send Jeremy into a panic. He looked back to the flat just as Amelia turned a light on and closed his eyes with a sigh of relief.

chapter 8

As she placed a kettle on the stove, Amelia's phone rang, startling her, in the silence. Her heart racing, she picked up. "Hello."

"Hi."

"Jeremy?" She walked over to the window to see him still outside.

"Yes. I just wanted to make sure you got in okay. And if you need anything at all please call me, no matter the time."

"Thank you. Goodnight." She waved.

"Goodnight." He waved back and drove away.

The kettle whistled and Amelia hurried to the kitchen after it. She made her cup of tea, completely unaware that a man in a solid black suit was standing outside her glass kitchen door, staring at her. He made no motion to get into the house. He was simply watching, and he didn't take his eyes off her. Not for one minute.

After adding a healthy amount of brandy to her tea, Amelia sat down at the dining room table, which had nothing on it, besides her father's letter. She sipped from her warm mug, eyeing the envelope, weary of what the contents might be—knowing that this was the moment she was meant to uncover it. After a few minutes of consideration, Amelia opened the letter. She looked at her father's handwriting, then she caught the smell of his aftershave. She brought the letter up to her nose, taking in the memory.

Suddenly, she was concerned that the scent would dissipate and that was all she had left. She placed the letter on the table before her, as if not touching it or taking in the scent would somehow preserve it. The man in the black suit watched her carefully as Amelia settled into her chair and began to read.

> *Dear Amelia,*
>
> *I knew someday I would probably have to explain all this, but I prayed that day would never come. I hope that you can forgive me. It was only out of love for you and my hope that you would lead a carefree life that I've held on to so many secrets for so long.*

The hairs on the back of Amelia's neck stood up and she stopped reading. She turned around to a large window behind her. She felt the presence of the man. She knew that she was being watched. She got up and closed the curtains, all the while telling herself that she was just being paranoid. She failed to realize, however, that she wasn't paranoid at all, but intuitive, and that she'd closed the curtains to the wrong window. The man in the black suit was still watching her.

Amelia returned to the letter, somehow at ease by concealing herself in behind the drapery.

> *Your mother had some of the most advanced abilities of any Witch ever recorded. Part of the role she assigned herself was to create a world-wide network of Witches so they could learn from each other, compile history and traditions, protect each other and progress within themselves and in the world. I know this will come as a shock to you, but her primary contact in the UK was my friend and your boss, Jeremy Roth.*

Amelia stared at the page, not sure she had read it correctly.

Her primary contact in the UK was my friend and your boss, Jeremy Roth.

Yes. That's what it said. It said that, in all the distance they had traveled, and in all the studies Amelia had focused on with the intention of staying away from Witchcraft, that she had gone nowhere at all! It said that the closest person to family she had left in the world had been lying to her for her entire life; that Jeremy Roth was not who he appeared to be at all; that he was a Witch. That's what it said. Amelia's chest tightened. She could feel the rage building inside of her, but she held it back, sipped her tea, and continued to read.

They wrote frequently and, when he had not heard from your mother over a period of a few months, Jeremy phoned our store in San Francisco. You may remember your mom's best friend, Summer. I gave her all our property and everything in it. So, when Jeremy called, she answered and told him what had happened. She also told him exactly what I'd instructed her to tell everyone—that you and I were not, in any way, a part of Wicca or Witchcraft any longer and not to contact us. Unfortunately, she also told him where we had gone and that we were practically neighbors.

Jeremy denied my request and came to the house just when we'd finally settled in. His reasons, he kept to himself at first, but when he realized that I would never let a Witch into your life, he brought me the correspondence between him and your mother.

In her last letter to him, Grace said that she knew she would be the next victim of The Organization. She had discovered a rogue group within them—not Witch hunters, but men of black magic, who were seeking the powers of a strong and pure Witch. These were men who believed they could harness the natural magick and power of another for their own purposes. Your mother knew they would want her eliminated from your upbringing so that, when you came of age, you would be without training and influence—a pure power. She knew this because The Organization had determined what your mother always believed to be true. That you are, in fact, the girl in the legends—that it is not just a story, but a record of the truth. That you, Amelia, are "The One."

The planetary alignments for your 28th birthday match exactly and the magickal abilities you exhibited as a small child were unheard of. Because of this, your mother had great hope for you, but she also feared for your safety. I couldn't ignore the letters, but I did not want to jump to any conclusions either. I knew that if your mother was right about who you were, or even if anyone thought she was right, eventually people would come looking for you, people who would hurt you. But I also knew that wouldn't happen until your 28th birthday and I wanted to give you a chance at a normal life. I wasn't convinced that you were the girl in the legend or, for that matter, that the legend was even a reality.

Jeremy and I finally came to an agreement. He would never speak to you about Wicca or The Craft, but he would keep me informed of any cautions. He would become a part of our lives—a friend. And he did. Jeremy and I became rather social as time passed. I had an interest in art and architecture and, because of that, you and I were always invited to The National Gallery's special exhibits and gala events. It was Jeremy's position that we expose you to the art that you've come to love so much.

Over the years, the dangers posed by The Organization seemed to lessen. At times we wondered if in fact you were in any danger at all. A Witch who is unaware and unpracticed, is also unthreatening, we thought. That is not to say that Jeremy did not want to teach you. He knew that you had unrealized talents that were quite extraordinary, but it was my wish that you live a normal childhood and he honored that.

When I fell ill, last spring, the doctors said it was cancer. Then they changed their minds; and then they changed their minds again. The truth is, they couldn't determine what was wrong. That is why I never told you what they said.

After a while, Jeremy and I began to suspect that my illness was not one any medical doctor could heal. With the coming of your 28th Birthday, Samhain and the Full Blood Moon, we realized that this was the beginning. The descendants of both the High Priestess Maeve's good magick and High Priest Domhall's evil spell were watching us, and so was The Organization.

The Witches are of no worry yet. The concern with them will come on the night of your birthday, when the moon is closest to the earth. That is when you will come into this power if you are in fact "The One." The goal of the opposing Witches, following your ancestor's bloodline, is to confirm that you are "The One," and then kill you before your power reaches its full potential on November the 1st. If you are "The One," and if they succeed, they will have won the Civil War of the Witches. If you are "The One" and they don't succeed, then you will exist with the greatest magickal strength and intuition the world has known since the Pharaohs ruled Ancient Egypt. That is the last time a female Witch had her twenty-eighth birthday under this particular planetary alignment.

The Organization is another matter altogether. As a whole they are still Witch hunters who show no mercy. They simply seek and destroy, but the rogue group within them now runs The Organization and their goal is not to kill you, but to control you; to gain control in the world by using your magick to satisfy their self-serving goals and need for power. It is a complicated task, for which they have spent your lifetime planning; a task that Jeremy and I believe they are setting in motion by casting a death spell on me. I am the last of your family, making me the last thing standing between you and The Craft.

The Organization wants you to practice now, Amelia. They want you to test your skills and develop them, not too much, but just enough, so that they can study you, so that they can determine just how to control you before you come into your power; so that when you do, they will actually control "The Ultimate Power" that "The One" is said to have.

*We don't know how they intend to do this but, as I said, we
believe they have been planning this your entire life.*

*I know this is a bit overwhelming, but with all of that
said, there is one more thing I must tell you. It is the most
difficult thing I have to write because I know how painful it
will be for you to read.*

*Jeremy and I are fairly certain that Wolfgang's death was
not an accident, but a hit by The Organization; again, to
place you in a position of being alone—in a position where
all you had left was The Craft, so that you wouldn't be distracted and would exercise your power without any influence
or support from outside forces.*

Amelia closed her eyes to swallow the sharp pain that came
over her. She had somehow held it together enough to read the
letter, but with these words about her Wolfgang, Amelia began to
cry. She was frustrated. All of her healing wounds were fresh again.
I can't do this all over again. She pounded her fists down on the
table. *Why is he telling me these things?* She pounded again and
again with growing fury. *Why is this something I have to know?*
Tears poured. *I can't do this. I just can't.*

Amelia pulled back and looked to the letter. She was almost
to the end, but she didn't want to read it. She didn't want to hear
any more … but she knew that she had to, so she continued as she
sobbed and her heart pounded with rage.

*The Witches are not easy to identify, but I suspect you
will sense when someone nearby intends to do you harm. The
men of The Organization are much different. They're stealthy,
strong, and organized. They are only seen when they want to
be, although they are not known to hide. You will know them
by their solid black tailored suits and the black town cars
that all of them drive. These are two groups of very powerful
people Amelia. They can not be ignored.*

*Jeremy has watched over you with the care and concern
of a father since you were seven-years-old. You can trust in
him as much as you ever trusted your mother and me. I can't*

imagine how you feel hearing all of this at once. I didn't know what else to do. I'm sorry. Jeremy is a good man. Please have faith in him. Please let him guide you. I love you, forever.
—Daddy

Amelia was filled with a frustration and anger that she could not begin to wrap her head around. It was all too much. *Did they plan my whole life so carefully that I wasn't even aware of it? Do I really love art? Under more honest circumstances would I have ended up a doctor or a lawyer?* She didn't have those answers and she knew that they didn't really matter. They didn't matter because this was the place she'd arrived at. This was the new reality that life had kicked her into and she would deal with it the same way she had so many times before. That's what she told herself. Now she just had to process what she'd read. So she poured another cup of tea, more brandy than tea this time, and sat back down to read the letter again. She had to be sure the words that she thought she read were the words that were actually there.

The man in the dark suit continued to watch her every move, her every emotion, and her every tear with the kind of patience that would make a normal person's skin crawl. It was as though he were watching a lab rat in a cage, just waiting for the right moment to begin the next step in the experiment; to twist the knife in the already tormented girl, if for no other reason, than to see just what would happen.

chapter 9

October 24, Seven Days to the Full Blood Moon

Amelia stepped outside the next morning to find herself surrounded by the fog that London is so famous for. She knew people hated it and got lost in it, but she hid within it. She'd always loved the element of mystery and surprise that it brought to the city's daily life. She got into her black BMW Roadster and hit the gas, driving much too fast for the weather conditions, but not thinking twice about it. She navigated on instinct, on the edge. This was how Amelia taunted the Grim Reaper on occasion, daring him to take her away.

* * *

Amelia moved through the halls of The National Gallery with purpose; everyone she passed noticed. No one even dared to say hello. Not one person on the staff had ever seen her so angry and each breathed a sigh of relief that they weren't the one she was gunning for as she whisked by.

She stopped at the open door to Jeremy's office, where he sat behind his desk, reading. He sensed her presence, but had no intention of looking up until he was ready. It was a power play that he frequently used when faced with an argument. It had diffused situations in the past, making them wait; making his attacker take another moment to think about what they were about to say or do; giving them a moment to reconsider. He finally looked up at Amelia and knew, instantly, that this tactic would not work on her. Not today.

"What the fuck did you do?" she asked in a tone seemingly delivered by the devil himself.

"I know it's a lot," he replied in a calm and direct manner, angering Amelia even more.

"You know it's a lot? It's insane!"

"It's true. All of it."

"You convinced my father that I was some sort of Wiccan messiah? That I not only have the power to bring down the "evil" Witches, but also to destroy this group of right-wing religious fanatics who have been executing Witches for a thousand years? 'The One' is a bedtime story!"

"And a rather horrifying one, don't you agree?" he asked, without raising his voice that was now tinted with arrogance.

"You're mocking me?"

"No. I think we've reached a point where we need to be clear and direct."

"Oh. I'm sorry. *Now* we've reach a point where we need to be clear and direct. Never mind the past twenty years!"

"The Organization is very real Amelia. You know that."

"Everybody knows that, but that doesn't mean I'm going to wipe them out like some sort of supernatural terminator. And with what? A magic wand?"

"That's not exactly what I had in mind."

"They've become an accepted institution of lunatics, for Christ sake. They're right up there with the all-cult favorites ..." She stopped yelling and stared straight into his eyes, almost penetrating his soul with her hurt and unforgiving tone. "... they're right up there with you. My boss. My friend. The Witch ... did it ever once occur to you to tell me?"

"Many times," he said, returning the merciless stare, infuriating Amelia even more.

Why is he always so even? So calm? It's almost patronizing, the way he's sitting there looking at me. The smug son of a bitch! Well, he wins!

"Bloody Hell!" she screamed. "You're supposed to be my friend! You're supposed to be the one to support me when I need it and you've been lying to me my entire life!"

"Because your father asked me to. I would never do anything to hurt you."

"Well you're a very good liar, sir. Too good, as far as I'm concerned. I feel like I don't even know you."

"Only because …"

She was too angry to let him finish. "Yes! My father! My father made you do it! He made you betray me, and now, thanks to you, he died thinking that he did something wrong. Thinking that his only child's life was in grave danger and there was nothing he could do about it. You're a prick, Jeremy. A certifiable son of a bitch. He was your friend! How could you have done such a thing?"

"Your father died relieved, knowing he was doing something right … I'm here to help you, Amelia. To guide you through what you're up against."

"I'm not up against a goddamn thing. I'm not going to open Pandora's Box for you."

"It's already open. What you need to do now is accept that and catch up," he said firmly.

"I'm not revolving my life around folklore, Jeremy."

"Neither am I."

"I've lost both my parents and my husband. And now some grave robber has my father."

"I appreciate that."

"I don't think you do," Amelia started out the door. Jeremy stood up, his demeanor forceful and unforgiving.

"Your father didn't just die Amelia. He was murdered." His direct delivery stopped Amelia short, but she did not turn to him. He walked slowly toward her, with great empathy. "And it wasn't just a grave robber; it was your enemies who took him." His tone softened as he came up behind her. "The same enemies who took Wolfgang from you. The people in your life have all died for the same reason. I know you haven't forgotten what happened in the park that night. What you're capable of."

Amelia's hands began to shake. She wanted to run, but she couldn't move, and where would she go? It was all she could do to hold herself up while she stared down at the floor. "Of course I haven't forgotten," she whispered, "as much as I would like to. I remember everything about that night and, on a bad day, I can even remember what it felt like, standing there while my own mother was murdered in front of me. That's not the kind of thing you forget," Amelia said as she began to cry once more. "No matter how hard you try." She closed her eyes in an attempt to hold her tears in, but she couldn't.

Jeremy put his arms around her. "I do know what I'm capable of, but just because I'm able to do it, doesn't mean I'm willing to," Amelia finally turned around and let herself fall into Jeremy's arms. "It's not fair."

"I know."

"You're all I have left. Why did you keep so many secrets from me? How am I supposed to trust you?"

"I'm sorry ... I'm so sorry."

"I can't do it. I won't. I don't want anything to do with The Craft."

"I know ... but I'm afraid you don't have a choice."

Amelia pulled back from Jeremy and pushed him away. That's not what she wanted to hear. *Why couldn't he have just lied?* Even if it was just for a minute? One minute. That's all she wanted. A moment of comfort. A moment that felt safe. A break for God's sake. Without another word or even looking at him, Amelia left Jeremy's office, letting the door slam behind her.

chapter 10

The blood rushed from Amelia's face and her hands began to go numb as she walked down the hall. She hurried into her office and quickly closed the door behind her. *Oh God.* She took a deep breath, grabbed a garbage can and began to vomit. She sunk down to the floor in a cold sweat.

Oh God. This is really happening. I'm really going to have to do this.

Amelia was frantic. She wasn't exactly sure of what she needed to do, but this began with her mother, so she decided it was her mother she should turn to for guidance.

She looked over at a large wooden chest on the opposite side of the room. To the common man it was a prize piece from a museum's collection of Egyptian artifacts, but, actually, it was a customized gift—crafted by her father in celebration of her decision to pursue a career in art and anthropology. Carved on it was the story of *Isis and the Seven Scorpions.*

"The box," he'd said, "is for all of your future treasures. It's to represent your new beginnings of greatness in the art world, just as the works of ancient Egypt represented significant and new beginnings in art and the world so many years ago."

Amelia was continually impressed by the attention to detail and thought put into this empty box of future treasures and deeply touched by the unsaid meaning of the gift. Using Isis was her father's way of including her mother in the gesture and in Amelia's future. Isis was a mother of magick and magick was all that Grace wanted to teach her child, something she had fallen short of during her most recent life.

Isis had also been Grace's chosen Goddess to call upon during rituals, bringing even more meaning to the gift. It was a symbol of protection, of new beginnings and of remembrance. It represented the essence of who Grace was and who Amelia could, one day, be. Perhaps that is why Amelia found it to be the naturally appropriate place to store the personal tools of her mother's Craft; tools that her father had taken so much care in making for her. Amelia had secretly packed them the night before she and her father moved from San Francisco to London. She had her mother's Book of Shadows, ritual candles, the recipes for her favorite incense, incense that she had never burned and all of her magickal tools. The Coven thought the Book of Shadows and magickal tools had been buried along with Grace's body, as was the tradition. William thought that they had been left at the house along with everything else. No one knew Amelia's secret.

She wiped her mouth and let go of the garbage can. Then she crawled across the floor and opened the chest. With the strong smell of incense and oils that poured out of it, it was as though her mother had stepped into the room with her. It smelled like home.

Amelia's eyes welled with tears, but she talked herself out of letting even one fall. *I've cried enough for a lifetime and I've got too much to do to get emotional.* She removed two black velvet bags and a small address book. The book was a kind of personal, worldwide Coven directory.

"Ah, here we go," she looked up Jeremy Roth. "There you are. You bastard. Mom's primary contact in London." Amelia continued to turn the pages of the book, carefully looking for a first name, knowing that she would recognize the last when she came to it. She stopped when she found the name of the woman she knew her mother would turn to if she were in this situation, "Summer Karlsen."

Summer was Grace's best friend and fellow practitioner of The Craft. She'd been like a second mother to Amelia, although Amelia's most significant memory of Summer was of her screams. The last time she'd seen her, she was soaked in Grace's blood. She couldn't picture her beyond that. With twenty years having passed, Amelia only hoped that she could find her and that she would be willing to help. If she was to trust anyone, it would be Summer.

Amelia took a deep breath, got up and sat down at her desk. She dialed Summer's number, becoming very nervous as the phone began to ring. After four rings she started to hang up when a man answered. "Hello."

"Yes. Hello. I'm looking for Summer. Summer Karlsen."

"You have the wrong number."

"Oh, right. I'm sorry," Amelia hung up the phone, almost relieved. She put the book down. "If you don't believe, it can't hurt you ..." She closed her eyes. "I don't believe in Witches. I don't believe in The Craft," she told herself, as if saying those words out loud would somehow make her new reality disappear.

"Moving on," she said in an attempt to change her mindset. Amelia picked up some sample invitations for the, "All Hallows Eve Gala, Presenting Francisco Goya" and looked them over, but the idea of work only lasted for a moment. She was too pent-up to focus. She needed to deal with the issue at hand. She needed to find her father's body.

She knew that it was close. She knew that where he'd been taken was related to Witchcraft. And she thought that, if she could clear her mind enough to step back and look at the situation from a distance, then the answer would be right in front of her.

I'll go for a walk, she decided. That's what Amelia did when she needed to think something through, or just empty her mind of thoughts so she could re-evaluate her situation and approach it with a clear head. She'd walk the streets of London until she was guided to the answer, something she'd done many times before. She'd walk and walk and walk until the answer of what to do was right in front of her.

Amelia stepped out of the Trafalgar Square entrance of the Gallery and decided to head toward the apple market in Covent Garden. The street performers and vendors peddling their crafts were always a nice distraction. As she walked down the Gallery steps, Amelia heard music and stopped in her tracks. It was Beethoven, but it wasn't a piano and it wasn't a recording. She looked around then followed the music across The National Gallery plaza and down the steps leading to the fountains in the center of Trafalgar Square. There she found a young German man playing an electric guitar. He had white blonde hair that almost reached his shoulders—hair that would be called "unkept" for a business man, but that almost defined a true musician. Hair like Wolfgang's.

When he finished the song, he looked up from his guitar to Amelia, revealing his ice blue eyes. She was frozen—a deer in headlights as they made eye contact. The young man seemed to look through her, seeing not only her face, but every aspect of who she was. Then, he simply looked back to his guitar and began to play again ... he began to play Beethoven's "Pastoral."

Amelia was overwhelmed. She just stood there looking at him, wondering why this man who looked so strikingly similar to her late husband was possessed to play that piece ... *their song* ... right in front of her, on a day when ... and then she realized ... Amelia hurried to the street where she flagged and taxi and jumped in.

chapter 11

Tears rolled down her cheeks, freely, as Amelia placed a bouquet of sunflowers over Wolfgang's grave. She'd always brought him sunflowers. It was the one flower that always made her smile—the only flower she thought smiled right back at her. And that was all she wanted for Wolfgang, wherever he was. A world of smiles. Amelia also wanted his help. Something had lead her to his gravesite and she would wait there until she knew why.

Mr. Paskin watched her from the distance. His wife had asked about little Amelia Pivens, "What will that poor girl ever do?" she'd said to her husband. "What does a child do when everything that is dear to her has been taken away? Do you think she'll love again?" she'd asked.

Mr. Paskin hadn't known how to respond. This was a girl he'd come to know only through her many tragedies. All he knew was that he hoped so. He hoped this girl, just beginning her time in this world, could find the ability to love again, to smile from the inside rather than force the facade on the outside.

"I miss you," Amelia said as she ran her hand over Wolfgang's name. "I wish you were here right now. I wish you could tell me a joke," she laughed as if he just had, remembering all the times he had her on the floor in stitches.

As she relaxed in her memories of him, something occurred to her. She again looked at his name, carved in the stone before her. She removed her mother's address book from her purse and turned to the inside of the front cover where all Grace's personal numbers were listed. Amelia's eyes fell on the number for "The Shop." She looked back to Wolfgang's gravestone. "Thank you."

Her hand shook as she dialed. With only three numbers left, she stopped dialing suddenly and scanned the graveyard. She'd felt something, someone watching her. It was the same feeling she'd had so many years ago in the Japanese Tea Garden, but again, she saw nothing.

And again, there was someone—someone in the distance watching her ... detailing her every move.

She looked back to her phone and took a deep breath. *Just dial, Amelia!* She did and, as the phone began the first ring, a woman answered. "Good Morning, The Shop."

"Hello, is this ..." she froze. It wasn't just that she couldn't find the words; her anxiety level was so high that it was as though she'd forgotten how to speak.

"Yes? Are you there?"

"Yes. I'm here. My name is Amelia Pivens Kreutzer and ..." She stopped talking. Again there was silence on the line. She'd just realized what she was about to say ... *and what?* She thought. *This woman is going to think I'm crazy.* "I'm sorry, I actually think I have the wrong number."

"No, you don't," the voice on the other end said, sending a rush through Amelia's entire body. "It's me, Amelia. It's Summer."

Amelia didn't say anything. She was afraid that if she opened her mouth she might vomit again. Summer was patient and quiet in waiting for Amelia to respond. Her voice cracked with nervousness when she finally did.

"I'm not sure I want to be doing this and I'm not sure I believe in it anymore ... but, I don't think I have a choice." She hit her forehead with the palm of her free hand, not believing these words were actually coming out of her mouth. "I know you really don't know me at all, but I need help with something. Someone murdered my husband three years ago, on my birthday. My father died unexpectedly last week and now his body is missing from the funeral home … and if my mother was right about who I am, then this is all because of me and I need your help."

Amelia's increasing anxiety brought on another wave of nausea. She struggled to hold it back, the sting burning the back of her throat. "I need to … Oh, God," she said.

Then she finally revealed the purpose of her call and it was clear to both women that the words Amelia spoke were the most difficult words of her life, "Summer, I called you because I need to know if I am 'The One' and I need you to help me re-enter The Craft."

chapter 12

Amelia took the following day off from work, which did not go unnoticed as it was such a rare occurrence. No one thought much of it, with her father's body missing; no one, besides Jeremy. Amelia walked down Monmouth Street, Grace's address book in hand. She stopped to double-check the cross street. Her mobile phone rang. Caller ID told her it was The National Gallery and she knew what that meant.

"Good Morning Jeremy," she said, while continuing to walk.

"Good Morning. I understand you've taken a personal day."

"Yes, but if there's something with the exhibit that I need to be there for, I'll come in."

"No everything is fine. It's just that you so rarely take a day off. I wanted to make sure you were alright."

"With my father missing I just need ..."

"I understand. So, you're at Scotland Yard with Detective Carlisle?" Jeremy asked, knowing full well she wasn't.

"I left him a message and I know they're looking, but I really wanted to take today just to be alone. To rest. To ..."

"To explore who you are?" he asked with both hope and caution.

"No. I'm not ready yet."

"You'll need to be. Samhain is coming quickly."

"Yes."

"And wherever your father is, it will be through your abilities that we find him. There's nothing that Scotland Yard can do, Amelia."

"I understand."

"I don't think you do."

Amelia said nothing. It was a conversation she did not want to have.

"His body will not be revealed until Samhain or the morning after," Jeremy continued. "That was the point of them stealing it."

"Who?"

"I can't be sure, but until Samhain you must focus on yourself. The kind of jeopardy you're facing is unknown. It's something that none of us understand. We need time together. Time for you to become comfortable with who you are."

Amelia did not respond and Jeremy wasn't surprised. She didn't want to commit to anything that she didn't completely understand. She never did. Amelia was a creature of habit and he knew her inside and out. He also knew exactly what she was doing on her day off and he had a pretty good idea of where she was, which irritated him.

"Alright, then," he said firmly, "listen to me now. The way to approach this is together. Going out on your own to research and explore something you haven't been involved with for twenty years is dangerous. The various Covens, good and bad, and The Organization are out there waiting. If you encounter someone who is intuitive enough to guide you, then they'll know you. They'll take you in through your scattered emotions and you'll find yourself at their mercy. You have no idea who your enemies are and you won't know them until it's too late. This is not a piece of art you're looking in to—it's a way of life and it's your heritage and, for all the interested parties, Amelia, it's personal."

"What are you saying?"

"I'm saying you don't understand who you are and I will be the one to teach you. Seeking out a local Coven meeting and popping in, thinking that you'll be safe and learn something by being a fly on the wall isn't going to work. You can't do that. I will give you books, information, practice—anything and everything to help you Amelia. But it has to be me and it has to be now. We haven't time for you to ease yourself into this."

She hated that Jeremy intuitively knew what she was up to, but she wanted more time so she didn't mind bending the truth for the moment to pursue things her way.

"Okay," she said as she stopped walking. A sign that read "Mysteries" was now directly in front of her, "but seeking out other Witches is not what today is about for me." The display window was filled with crystals, jewelry and books on The Craft. She took in the smell of incense drifting from inside. Her head tingled and her senses were overtaken with lovely memories of her childhood in San Francisco.

"I'm very serious about this Amelia. It's for your own well-being," Jeremy continued. Amelia closed her eyes, allowing herself to let the familiar scent take over her body.

"I appreciate that," she said, finding herself feeling very at ease.

"And, we have a very serious time-line we're working with. Take today to rest and we'll start tomorrow, alright?"

"Tomorrow is fine."

"And you won't go snooping around local Covens today? Today is for rest?"

"Today is for peace of mind," Amelia said as she hung up and turned off her mobile phone, then walked through the front door of Mysteries.

* * *

"Here we go," Jeremy said to himself as he hung up the phone, wondering what kind of trouble Amelia was about to get herself into. Wondering exactly where she was and knowing that she'd decided to research The Craft on her own. Wondering if she was at Mysteries and, if she was, exactly what she would find there. She was a smart young woman. She always had been, and that's what amazed Jeremy about her actions. He was worried that she was going to attack the subject the same way she did when she was researching a piece of art. He worried that she had not fully grasped that she was dealing with a delicate life-and-death situation; that there was a potential for this to escalate into one of those great stories of passion and destruction that every religion has. One wrong move could lead to a series of events that could get them both killed.

Jeremy did love Amelia like a daughter, but like a father, he was going to have to step back and let her fall this time. All that he could do now was wait and hope. Hope that, by the end of her day, Amelia would realize that with such little time, his help was the only way she was going to make it through the coming of Samhain, her birthday and the Full Blood Moon. He didn't want to force her. He knew that he couldn't. *She'll figure it out by the end of the day*, he told himself. *I just hope she doesn't find herself in a world of hurt before that.*

* * *

Amelia stood at the register with a selection of magazines, *New Witch*, *Witchcraft and Wicca,* and *Pentacle*. She also had a Celtic charm that she'd picked up, for no reason in particular. It was a Briar Rose and it had caught her eye while she was wandering through the shop.

"Will that be all?" the girl behind the counter asked.

"Yes," she answered as she looked up from her purse to the girl and saw not her, but a drawing hanging on the wall just behind her. Amelia was taken back by the image. The girl noticed, but said nothing. She'd grown accustomed to strange occurrences in the shop and she knew if Amelia had something to say, she would.

"Who is that?"

The girl turned around to the small drawing. "I don't know. I think a woman who used to do readings here did that. She did quite a bit of sketching. Sometimes she would hang them here."

"That's an old one."

"Yeah. I guess it is," the girl said as she looked closely. "The edges are kind of yellow."

"So you don't know who the woman in the drawing is?"

"No … Do you?"

"She just looks like someone."

The girl nodded her head as she looked from Amelia to the drawing and back again. "She looks like you."

"A little bit."

"A lot actually," she said to Amelia with a strange feeling of connection and curiosity coming over her.

"Yes," Amelia said in a manner that let the girl know the conversation was now over. The girl was young, but she'd worked at Mysteries long enough to understand.

"Cash or charge?"

"Cash," Amelia handed the girl exact change. "Have a good day."

"Thanks. You too."

Amelia stepped out on to Monmouth Street, shoving her purchase deep down into her bag. The drawing had unnerved her. It made her realize that there were, in fact, many things she didn't understand.

Maybe I should have listened to Jeremy, she thought as she wondered if the drawing was of who it appeared to be. If the woman was, in fact, her mother. *But why would a drawing of my mother be hanging on the wall here? She never traveled overseas ... But she did create this network and she also owned a shop catering to The Craft ... and Mysteries is in her address book. Maybe someone else there sent letters back and forth, too. That's it. Someone who worked there then had been part of the network. That makes sense.*

As Amelia pondered and reasoned in this conversation with herself, she whisked right by Detective Carlisle, completely oblivious. He was sitting in an unmarked car, with his mid-morning latte, from Caffè Nero, watching her.

He watched her disappear down the street and the detective felt drawn to her. Not just sexually, but to her being. And although nothing had transpired between them, the mere notion of Amelia made him feel as if he were committing adultery. There was something different about her that he couldn't place. She was beautiful and obviously broken, but through no fault of her own. She was fragile in a way that drew him in. Her black hair, snow white skin and green eyes seemed to embody her tragedies, but still her beauty was unparalleled.

Detective Carlisle turned his eyes back to Mysteries. *So she's a Witch.* It made sense to him. She certainly wasn't the first one he'd encountered in his fourteen years at Scotland Yard. *That's the secret. That's why they wouldn't talk. But who steals the body of a Witch?* That was a question that the detective had not encountered before. He finished off his coffee and got out of the car to eavesdrop on any gossip the girls behind the counter at Mysteries might be having about young Mrs. Amelia Pivens Kreutzer.

chapter 13

October 26, Five Days to the Full Blood Moon

The following morning Amelia was tired. She'd spent the afternoon reading and stayed up well into the night on the internet. She'd read the magazines from front to back, then over again. As Jeremy suspected, she wanted to do all she could to familiarize herself with the current beliefs and the mindset of the modern Witch. Beyond that, she wanted the pulse of the Witches who lived in London. She wanted to know where the shops were, where the meetings were and how someone new to The Craft could become involved. She wanted to remember everything she'd forgotten and she wanted to pack a lifetime's worth of knowledge into one day.

As Amelia and Jeremy walked through the East Wing of the Gallery, she noted the connections between Goya's approach to his work and the Wiccan approach to life—honest, with plenty of opinions, but no judgment.

"It's exciting isn't it? Your exhibit. I wasn't sure you would pull it off and I never thought it would happen so fast," Jeremy finally said, interrupting Amelia's daydream-like state.

"I'll take that as a compliment."

"As you should."

Amelia and Jeremy checked the area where workmen were busy replicating the various rooms of *Quinta del Sordo*, the home

in which Goya lived out his final days and where he painted and
displayed the famous collection of *Black Paintings*. Amelia watched
the men as if it were her own home they were building. It brought
Jeremy back to the first time Amelia saw Goya's work and he found
himself in a rather sentimental moment.

"What?" she smiled.

"Little Amelia," he said, "why do you think he surrounded
himself like this? With every wall of his house painted with such
brutal works?"

They walked over to a set of plans representing how Goya's
house was constructed and where each of the paintings hung.

"What do I think or which critic do I agree with?"

Jeremy gave her a look, inviting her to answer whichever question she liked, or both.

"I think he wanted to surround himself with the truth—of
himself and of the world."

They continued walking through the exhibit and into another
room where a few pieces had already been hung.

"Why?"

"Because it's something we don't want to face and, usually,
can't help but know if it's placed directly in front of us."

"Why not live the lie, happily, among other rich men?"

Amelia's gaze fell on Goya's *Road to Hell*, a swirl of chaos where
four people are falling into the depths of hell surrounded by the
vengeful creatures that inhabit it. "Because he couldn't. That kind
of life didn't contradict what he wanted, it contradicted who he
was."

Amelia turned to Jeremy, trying to figure out the motivation
behind their conversation. "Are you trying to have me compare
my opinion of Goya's views with my own life?"

"You made the observation."

"That you led me to."

"Guided. That I guided you to."

Amelia and Jeremy heard footsteps behind them and turned
around to see Claude approaching with a beautiful, mother-earth
type woman in her early 50s. She had blue eyes and long, blonde-

gray hair that fell just below her waist. Within a moment of her presence, Amelia found herself completely at ease.

"This is Summer Karlsen," Claude said as the woman took Amelia in an embrace.

"Aren't you beautiful? Just like your mother."

Summer extended her hand to Jeremy. "I'm Summer," she started to say as she realized who he was. Then, instead of shaking his hand, she gave him a big hug. "After all these years."

"Summer Karlsen."

"Jeremy Roth."

"You know each other?" Amelia asked, unable to hide her distress.

"You didn't tell him I was coming?"

"I suspected," said Jeremy.

"You did?" Amelia said, taken completely off guard.

"You were too mad to come to me, but I knew you needed to talk to someone. She was your mother's best friend—the obvious choice."

"Summer was the obvious choice?" Amelia said, truly shocked. Jeremy nodded.

Summer looked back and forth between them, unsure of exactly what she'd walked into, but determined to smooth it out. "So many secrets."

"And well-kept," Jeremy added. "It's only natural she feels hesitant."

"Yes," Summer said as she wrapped her arms around Amelia, "but we'll get you past that." Amelia didn't quite know what to say. "We all know each other and we all kept things from you. We didn't mean to be deceptive but wished only to protect you." Amelia remained silent. She felt trapped. "Your mom created a worldwide network so we could all support each other. It's amazing what she did. There's a contact in every city. Jeremy is London and, after your mother died, I became San Francisco. He's how I always knew you were okay."

"So you knew my father died?"

Summer nodded, "Yes. And I'd hoped you would call."

"You didn't mention this on the phone."

"It wasn't the right time." She took Jeremy's hand in hers. "We're here to guide you."

Amelia looked from Summer to Jeremy. She looked deep into his eyes, hoping that she could trust him, but not sure that she should—wanting to believe in him and this network of Witches and knowing there was not much of an alternative. Amelia decided to give Jeremy a chance.

"Alright," she said and let Jeremy give her a fatherly hug, "but I'm still mad at you."

"I know. It's getting late. Why don't you take Summer home and I'll finish up here."

"So tomorrow's the day," Amelia said with brave confidence and a much-needed willingness.

Jeremy kissed her forehead, "Yes. Tomorrow is the day little Amelia."

chapter 14

Summer and Amelia walked through the main doors of the museum and outside, on to Trafalgar Square. It was dark and the moon shone down on them as it danced off the fountains on either side of the tall memorial built in memory of Admiral Nelson, who won his final battle on the Spanish Cape of Trafalgar.

"It's a little bit colder than California," Summer said as she hugged her coat tight around her.

"Brisk. I love it," Amelia breathed in the cold air. "Everything is so clean and still, but so alive."

"It is."

Summer looked up and kissed two fingers as a sign of respect and acknowledgement to the moon. Amelia watched her. It reminded her of the day-to-day life of a Witch.

"Come on. Make a wish."

Amelia felt a bit reluctant; still unsure of the life she was being forced into.

"Do you remember how?"

Amelia made a fist then extended only her index and little fingers, so her hand resembled the head of a horned animal. She held it up to the moon and, from her point of view, it looked as if she were cradling the moon between the horns. She silently made her wish then lowered her hand.

"Feels good, doesn't it?"

"It's familiar, but still awkward."

"We're in the lunar cycle that's going to take us to your birth-day."

"And the biggest night of my career."

"The biggest night of your life," Summer added. "You know, the October moon is good for change and new things."

"I remember. And it's a good thing. I'm going to need all the help I can get."

"Mrs. Kreutzer," a voice called from behind. They turned around to find Martel.

"Please. It's Amelia. This is my friend, Summer Karlsen. Summer, Señor Martel Demingo."

"Hello."

Martel and Summer shook hands. When their eyes met they had an instant connection of some kind. A mutual moment of *deja vu*.

"It's nice to meet you, Señor."

"And you. Is this the way to the car park?" Martel asked, directing an interested, but respectful gaze on Amelia.

Summer noticed the attraction and Amelia's reserved interest.

"Yes. Walk with us," Amelia said.

"I get confused here."

"Everyone does. Too many exits."

"You're visiting, too?" Summer asked.

"Yes. From Madrid."

"Señor Demingo has been kind enough to loan us *The Prado*'s extensive Goya collection for a special exhibition."

"Wonderful."

"Will you be here for the opening, Ms. Karlsen?"

"Of course."

"Then you're here for a while. Are you here on business?"

"No, this trip is strictly pleasure."

* * *

Amelia spent the drive home from the museum filling Summer in on the last twenty years of her life, the primary focus of which was Wolfgang. Amelia pulled on to her street just as a black town car pulled away from her flat. She didn't notice because it left in the same direction she was driving, it had a bit of a lead on her and she was busy, rambling on to Summer. She was relaxed. It felt good talking with another woman—a mother figure and a best girlfriend all rolled into one. She'd had neither since she'd lost her grandmother.

"... I haven't been with anyone since Wolfgang. Señor Demingo is a lovely distraction, but I'm not ready yet. I don't know if I ever will be. Although it is always nice to be noticed."

"Try and let yourself enjoy it."

"There's no way," Amelia said. She couldn't imagine being in a relationship or even on a date. Not yet. And certainly not with the curator of the museum who was responsible for almost half of the art in her new exhibit. "Right now, my priority is understanding who has my father's body, why, and how I'm going to get it back."

"Once they've succeeded in causing you enough stress and fear, they'll begin work on pushing you to a point of desperation."

"I know."

"But know that. That's *all* it is, Amelia—a mind game. The Organization, the opposing Witches, they all have a respect for the dead. Fear of the other world keeps them all honest to a certain extent. I'm almost positive that your father's body is fine and being well-cared for, if only out of their own superstitions. He'll be returned on Samhain. They've taken him to wear you down, not to bring harm to him or his next life."

"Who's taken him?"

"I'm not sure yet, but we'll get there. I promise you that."

"I hope you're right."

"Don't just hope Amelia, know that I'm right. You've got to believe it. The strongest power we have now is your vision."

Amelia said nothing in response.

"What is it?"

"Nothing, it's just that ... It's all so unbelievable. This is the kind of thing you read about in a novel set five-hundred years ago in some ancient world—but it's all happening right now, right here, and I'm a part of it. It's real. No matter how you look at it, it's a lot and it's completely overwhelming."

"That's why I'm here."

"I'm so glad. Thank you."

They got out of the car and walked up the front steps to find the door slightly open. Amelia moved forward and Summer stepped back. "Call Jeremy," Summer said firmly.

Amelia pushed the front door open to see that her home had been ransacked.

"Now, Amelia!"

Amelia pressed a button on her mobile phone. As it began to ring, she handed it to Summer and started to walk inside. Summer took her arm and held her back. "No, Amelia. We'll wait for Jeremy."

chapter 15

Amelia rolled her wedding band nervously through her fingers as she checked to make sure that no photographs of her and Wolfgang had been taken or damaged.

"You're absolutely sure nothing is missing?" Jeremy asked as he surveyed the first floor of Amelia's flat for the second time.

"As sure as I can be, but there are holes in the walls. What were they looking for? What do they think I have?"

"Nothing. The Organization always leaves evidence to make things look like a common crime."

"So they weren't looking for anything?"

"No."

"Then what were they doing here?"

Summer became very still. She sensed something. She and Jeremy held a stare and he stopped moving too. The hair on Amelia's arms stood up. She could feel some kind of energy affecting her.

Jeremy started up the stairs. Summer took Amelia's hand and they followed. Jeremy stopped halfway up. "Can you smell it?"

"Incense," Amelia said simply, not understanding the significance of it.

Summer recognized the distinct scents, which clearly worried her. "It's John the Conqueror and Helping Hand incense. They've combined them."

"Yes, they have," Jeremy said, also recognizing the blend of smells as he continued up the stairs.

They reached the top and Amelia went toward her bedroom, while Jeremy and Summer followed the smoke to the bathroom. The door was open just enough to let it filter out into the house. Jeremy slowly pushed the door open, only to be overpowered by another smell, Bend Over Drops. The drops were a potent magickal oil and they were burning over a candle next to the incense. Summer gasped at the combination, just as Amelia pushed the door to her room open and shrieked, sending Jeremy and Summer rushing down the hall.

Amelia stood at her bedroom door, looking in on it; afraid to go beyond the threshold. The room was full of yellow and blue candles set in a circle around her bed. Black and white feathers covered her pillows. A panic rushed through all of them; then a puzzled and worrisome calm came over Summer and Jeremy. Jeremy went in and walked around, looking at what had been done. Amelia allowed herself to breathe and, as she soaked in what she saw before her, she realized it was somewhat familiar. "Yellow and blue are the candles of Scorpio. This is supposed to bring out the positive qualities in me, right?"

"That is correct," Jeremy said.

"Who would do that?"

Summer knew what she was seeing, but she was still trying to figure out why. "It's all positive reinforcements."

"Someone broke in to try and help me?"

With Amelia's words, Summer and Jeremy looked to each other. They didn't need to say anything to communicate their fear. In that moment they both knew what was happening. *They know.* Jeremy looked to Amelia, his demeanor serious and matter-of-fact. There was no longer time to entertain Amelia about what was expected of her. She would have to dive into the deep end and deal with who she was quickly and efficiently. "It's The Organization. No doubt. The feathers are for union and protection. A union with them and protection from the opposing Witches. The candles were placed to empower you and the incense and oil were combined as a tool to influence you. They want you strong and they want control. They know you've decided to re-enter The Craft. They want to stay by your side so that when the time comes they can make you their puppet."

"How do they know?"

"Knowing is their purpose."

"But it's a spell. You're sure it's not the other Witches? You're sure someone on our side isn't trying to help?"

Summer and Jeremy just looked at her, as if to say, don't fool yourself about this.

"Right. Okay, but it's The Organization, not the other Witches?"

Summer nodded her head, while Jeremy continued with his stern and formal manner.

"The opposing Witches wouldn't go to the trouble. They're just going to want you gone, but they'll wait. They'll wait for the moon."

"Right, of course," Amelia snipped with a blend of fear and sarcasm. "That makes sense. They wait for the moon. They'll wait for the goddamn moon! What are we talking about? What are we doing here? Group 'A' is going to control me and Group 'B' is going to strike me down? I don't think so. I've had enough."

"The men of The Organization are very well practiced," Jeremy said calmly as he started blowing out the candles, "and they completely lack morals. Their rogue group seeks power only for the sake of having it and the magickal abilities of these men can not be underestimated."

Summer gently took Amelia's arm. "You've got to let go of the confines and the structure of the world as it was taught to you after your mother died. It's much bigger than that. In Western Civilization they only teach what they can control. I know it's hard to understand, but it's time."

"Hard? Yes, it's hard, but as far as words go, 'madness' is the one that comes to mind. This is madness! I don't even know if I am 'The One' or if there is a 'One' and neither do you. It's been twenty-one years since that night."

"Enough!" Jeremy said with an authority that shook the room. "Eliminate those thoughts. You speak those words to try and convince yourself of what isn't. This is in your blood, Amelia. If you do not practice, they'll kill you. And if you do, you are giving us the first opportunity, in hundreds of years, to rid the world of the misguided Witches as well as The Organization and the rogue operatives within it. You are the only hope to stop the fighting forever and to balance the world's power as it is intended to be. There are no decisions to be made here. This is the reality of the way things are. You're going to have to get used to it and live by it from this point on. You can choose to ignore it, but that won't stop anything. Just look at your home, at what's been done here tonight. This is all very real and it's not going away. If you turn your back on what's coming you will gain nothing except confusion and danger when the Full Moon arrives."

Summer put her arms around Amelia. "I know that you're scared and reluctant, and we can't blame you for that, but do you remember what your mother used to tell you?"

Amelia was surprised at how quickly and clearly she did remember. "Once you come into your own, you won't have to search for the power. You will only need to realize it and then accept it with a pure heart and a focused mind."

"That's it. We're just trying to guide you through your realization, sweetheart. Jeremy's right. The magick and the history are already there. You can't stop it from coming through you. It's fate."

To the same degree that Summer approached Amelia as a mother, Jeremy approached her as a professor, a scientist and a military leader. He paced the room as if to take no prisoners.

"All living beings are inherently magick, Amelia. Your mother was right. It only needs to be realized for it to be. For most, their magick will never be known. For some, it will come more naturally than for others. And for a select few, it cannot be ignored. On Samhain, when the Full Blood Moon is closest to the earth and you enter your twenty-eighth year, you will find yourself with a realization that brings you above all others. Do you understand the gravity of that?"

"Yes."

Summer looked to Jeremy, her expression asking him to end the conversation. She knew Amelia had had enough. "She's okay."

Jeremy took the cue. "Fine then. Tomorrow night. We'll meet and we'll see where you are. A non-specific ceremony led by your intuition will give us an idea of what to expect on Samhain."

"I'm not sure I'm prepared. I ..."

Jeremy cut her off. "Did you not hear your own words? The words of your mother? You need only let yourself realize and believe. This is about confidence and having an open mind. The ability is already present within you."

"Yes, I know," she scanned the house. "Should we at least let Detective Carlisle know about this?"

"No," Jeremy said, then he kissed Amelia's forehead. "I know how I must sound, but I want nothing other than your well-being." He turned to kiss Summer on the cheek. "I'm glad you're here."

"Me too."

"I'll have a car for you tomorrow that you can drive during your stay. I keep a left-hand drive for my American guests. You're still on the wrong side of the road, but at least you can shift with greater ease."

"Thank you."

"Good night."

Amelia watched Jeremy drive away in his Rolls Royce, while Summer watched her—taking in her pain, her confusion, her distrust. "He comes on strong."

"Yes, he does. I love him, but he's lied to me my entire life and I'm just not comfortable with that."

"He had to Amelia ... For him, and for a lot of people, what's going on here is what their whole life has been about. It's hard for him to balance his parental feelings for you against the idea of saving all Witches from further persecution, now and for generations to come. I know that you think of yourself as just a girl, but the Witch that people believe you to be is unparalleled. You can't ignore that any more."

"I never ignored it. I never knew."

"Didn't you though?" Summer asked looking deep into Amelia's eyes.

chapter 16

Amelia set a kettle of water on the stove for tea. Summer watched her, wondering just how to approach the enormous task ahead of them. She tried to determine what was most important for Amelia to know before Samhain, then came to the conclusion that what was most important was ... absolutely everything. While she tackled her thoughts, her eyes darted around the room and eventually stopped on an old photograph of Amelia and Wolfgang having dinner at a café. Then she realized that the nook she was sitting in was a very similar setting to the one in the picture; same table, same chairs, vase, napkins and table cloth. Amelia and Wolfgang had re-created "their place" in Paris, in their kitchen at home as a second anniversary gift to each other. The photograph was a candid moment of Amelia and Wolfgang laughing; a story in and of itself that Summer journeyed into for just a moment ... and then it was Amelia who was watching her.

"If I had been given a choice, I would have done anything if they just would have let him live," Amelia placed a tray of tea on the table.

"And that's why you weren't given a choice." Amelia tensed at Summer's no-nonsense response, but said nothing. "Wolfgang's life was taken for a very specific reason."

"I still love him so much."

"And that's the reason."

"I suppose that makes sense in this demented scenario."

"Yes. Unfortunately it does." Summer shifted in her chair, not knowing exactly how to ask her next question, which was becoming increasingly important in regard to how to handle Amelia during her journey back into The Craft. "How do you deal with it?" she asked.

"What?"

"Him being gone."

Amelia sipped her tea, eyeing Summer over the rim of the cup, "No one ever asks me about that."

"I gather, but it is important."

"Why?"

"Because The Craft and Wicca are about balance and Wolfgang's presence in your life seems rather significant for someone who has been gone for three years."

"It is. It's very significant because I'm not ready for any more changes. I write him letters. I still talk to him. I try to work every hour that I'm awake ... I don't deal with it at all, really—to answer your question."

"You write him letters?"

"Yes."

"And where do you send them?" Summer asked, trying to pry the doors of Amelia's personal life open further.

"I can't do this right now. Is that okay?"

"Of course it is."

"It's just that ... he's not someone I'm willing to let go of. Not now. Not yet. And we have quite a few other things to deal with at the moment."

"We do."

"So these people ... these Witches and The Organization, they've been watching me my entire life?"

"Probably." Amelia sat down across from her. "What went on at that ceremony has been talked about ever since. You were so young. And the fact that every entity you summoned came is unheard of. In the history of all recorded Witchcraft and Wicca, nothing like that has ever happened, Amelia. There has also never been such a powerful Circle of Protection, swirling with magick, that wasn't closed." Amelia tilted her head forward, letting her hair fall over her eyes, feeling guilty and uncomfortable. "Your mother was killed. You ran away. No one closed the Circle or released the Quarters. A great deal of energy was left open to the universe—undirected energy that could prove to be dangerous." Summer sipped her tea. "Jeremy wasn't sure you were ready for this conversation."

"Ready, no? Willing, yes. But I'm willing to talk, not to be told. I won't be ordered around."

"No one wants to do that. Jeremy is just very intense."

"Well, he's too intense. This is still a lot. The Craft did kill my mother."

"No. A single person killed your mother. You've got to focus and accept the fact that she died because her time in this life was over. It's very important you understand that. You can't base your actions on personal feelings or revenge when you practice."

"I don't know if I'll ever be pure enough to do that. I don't know if I care either. I'm angry, Summer. I'm angry and I'm hurt and I have been for a very long time. I just want to give my father a proper burial and end this."

"Then they've got you right where they want you,"

Amelia sat back in her chair. She hadn't expected Summer to be so frank, but it didn't bother her. After the initial sting she found her honesty rather refreshing.

"Fighting with hate and selfishness brings out weakness. They're hoping that your rage will blind you from what's really happening. That you won't even see them coming. You've got to go after them by recognizing the Witch that you are and empowering yourself with the idea of worldly harmony and balance. They'll get what they deserve from the universe, in threefold, but the fate of others is not for you to decide. 'Harm None' is the only strict rule in all of Wicca and it is essential. If you don't live by it, you will exist only as a woman with dangerous abilities and insight. You will have no checks and balances. No good will come of it."

"I know. I'm just trying to be honest. You're basically proposing that I go up against two groups of people who have, between them, robbed me of my life and you're asking me to do it with a clear head and a pure heart for the betterment of the universe. I'm sorry, I'm just not that sure of myself and of my life and the world. You do realize that you're asking an awful lot of just one woman?"

"You are one woman, but what you have, Amelia, is a gift and it should be treated as such. What Jeremy and I are proposing is not what you've just described."

Amelia stared at Summer with a somewhat amused look that in a moment became serious. "Go on."

"Jeremy, the Witches in our network, and I are asking one thing of you—that you accept your blessing as 'The One,' if that is, in fact, who you are. We ask that you allow all 'The Ultimate Power' to infuse you, untainted, with proper universal balance, rather than with concern for personal gain or loss. You being 'The One' has nothing to do with the other people in your life who have suffered in the grand scheme of things. No one makes that connection besides you. Do you understand?"

Amelia nodded her head, again hiding her eyes behind her mop of black hair, just as she had as a child. Put that way, she did understand and she understood far more than she wanted to. "Tomorrow then."

"Tomorrow you go to work and you do what needs to be done for your Goya opening. It's important that you maintain your life as you created it. Then tomorrow night we'll go to Jeremy's and we'll do whatever comes naturally and feels comfortable for you."

"I don't need to prepare anything?"

"It's just a trial run, but a little homework never hurt anyone. Knowledge provides confidence. Everything else is locked away in that mind of yours and I'm hoping we will set it all free, just by us being together. I don't want to force anything. I think you should lead us with what feels right and we'll guide and support you as you go. You've got to listen to your instincts. That's the only way to find out what's really within you. It's all a matter of getting you to a place where stepping into your skin as a Witch and as 'The One' feels comfortable, or at least right, instead of confusing or stressful."

"And if I decide 'The One' isn't someone I want to be."

"You can't control fate, Amelia. The best you can do is embrace it and see it for the good it holds. You won't be giving up your art or your life. You will simply be adding another dimension to it." Summer got up, dug through her bag, and took out a homemade candle. "Got a match?"

Amelia handed her a book of matches and the smell of the candle reached her. "Coconut."

"It's yummy isn't it?"

"Is it for spiritual purification of the house?"

"Yes. And because it smells good. You have done some homework."

"I've done some reading, but that one I remember. I don't know why. I completely forgot until just now."

"It's amazing what smells can trigger."

"Thank you for coming."

"I'm glad you called."

"Summer …" she hesitated, "I'm scared."

"Of course you are, but I think after tomorrow night, you will feel better. That's why I'm here early. We've got time before the Full Blood Moon for you to play with your magick, to get used to who you are and to get comfortable with who you might be."

"Don't leave me okay?"

"I'm not going anywhere."

Amelia got up and surveyed the messy house. "So we're both in the guest room tonight."

"Slumber party," Summer laughed.

They both headed up the stairs, relieved to be together and completely unaware of the man, in a solid back suit, watching them from the window in the front room. After the lights went out he scrolled through the pictures on his digital camera, all the way back to the flat before it was broken in to. The man had been there all night.

chapter 17

October 27, Four Days to the Full Blood Moon

After a night of deep sleep, filled with dreams that she could not remember, Amelia sat in her office enjoying her morning coffee. She'd come in early to work, but found herself more interested in reading an information pamphlet on Witchfest, an upcoming two-day gathering in London for Witches from all over the world. The pamphlet had come as part of *Witchcraft & Wicca Magazine.* She thought she might go. That there might be a whole community out there which could get her more excited about her heritage ... *Or are they all just freaks trying to fill the holes in their lives with something they don't even understand?* she wondered. She hated to be cynical, but she couldn't help it and Amelia was often her own devil's advocate. *Are they commercializing Wicca and The Craft now? Like Christmas?* She laughed at the thought and then reconsidered it. *If there are so many people attracted to it that they are publishing competitive magazines, why not?* She sipped her coffee, searching her mind for an excuse to attend the festival. *So, what difference does it make if it's commercial? As long as it's a positive experience; one that I can draw something real from, something that's real for me.* That was it, she decided. She would go.

The gathering was scheduled for November 6th and 7th, just one week after Amelia's birthday. She could only wonder why they wouldn't schedule it for the night of Samhain and the Full Blood Moon. *Why schedule it for only one week later if not on the night? Is there a holiday I don't know about or … are they waiting for something? Oh, my God what if they are waiting?*

The thought rushed through her like wildfire as she considered the fact that she might be "The One." *If the festival is the week after Samhain because they're waiting for something, then they're waiting to see what the Full Blood Moon will bring …* She sat back in her chair. *Could that be right? Could all these people know? Could they all be waiting for me? To see if I'm her?* A wave of nausea began in her stomach and traveled up to her head and down through her knees. *That can't be right.*

Martel stood in the doorway watching her. She was too deep in her thoughts to notice or to try hiding her Witchcraft magazines when he finally realized there would be no right time and knocked.

"Hello there," she said, quickly snapping back to business.

"Señora, How are you?"

"Well, thank you. And you? Are you enjoying London?"

"Always."

"What can I help you with?"

"I was hoping I might have a meeting with your security staff."

"You're worried about the temporary construction we're doing for *The Black Paintings*."

"Of course. As you would be, I'm sure."

"I can't disagree."

"I've decided to stay in London through the first month of the exhibit, for my own peace of mind."

"The insurance company did sign off on the construction."

"I know that the structure is secure, and also that many liberties have been taken. The idea of temporary walls with temporary alarm systems holding a complete collection …" He blessed himself. "The insurance company is concerned with money, but can you really place a value?"

Amelia found it so endearing the way he cared for each painting that her grin completely covered her face, "They're your babies."

"Sí. I am happy that they will be in such an authentic setting, but I need a little more reassurance on their safety. Not just for *The Prado*, but for myself."

"I understand. Have you discussed this with Jeremy? He thinks of this place as his home and each piece of work a precious relative."

"Yes. For that he is known, as are you incidentally. Jeremy and I have talked, but ..." Martel trailed off, searching for the correct and most polite words.

"But?"

"The two of you watch over everything. The entire museum. I want to speak with the people who are assigned to be at a specific place on the floor. I want to know their names and their faces. It is Claude Benson and his team who will actually be watching. This is why I've come to request a meeting with them."

"I understand."

"It's all happening so fast."

"This is why I invited you to be a part of this exhibit over a year ago, Señor Demingo."

"I know."

"But I certainly understand and I want you to feel just as at home here as you do at *The Prado*."

"Thank you," he said glancing down at Amelia's desk where the Witchcraft magazines were out in plain view.

"Halloween research," she joked. "I get caught up in all the fantastic tales at this time of year."

Martel nodded, not quite believing her. "Witchcraft is one of the many interesting things England is known for."

A knock at the door disrupted the moment and they both looked over to find Detective Carlisle. "Sorry to come unannounced," he apologized.

"Detective Carlisle. Please. Come in," Amelia said, moving a file over the magazines, which Martel could not help but notice.

"I was just on my way out," Martel said as the detective walked in and the two men casually sized each other up; each wondering just who the other was and how closely he was connected to Amelia, both professionally and personally. It was a masculine moment that flattered Amelia, although she did want it over as soon as humanly possible.

"Claude left early, Señor Demingo. You can speak with him directly about a meeting tomorrow."

"Thank you," he said as he walked out the door, taking one more look at Detective Carlisle.

Amelia waited until Martel was out of earshot to address the detective. "You haven't found him yet, have you?"

"No, Madam. Can we take a walk?"

"Sure."

chapter 18

Detective Carlisle and Amelia walked down the front steps of The National Gallery. "Admiral Nelson," the detective said as he looked up at the memorial, where the Admiral stood on a post high above them. "He fought quite a few battles to get to this square—to merit the highest post right in the center of it so that he could look down on all of us like God."

"Yes, I suppose he did. Do you think they were all warranted?"

"What?"

"The battles."

"Warranted or not, they were battles that needed to be fought with honor."

Amelia said nothing, but she did not hide the fact that she didn't like his answer.

"Battles and war will never extinct themselves, Mrs. Kreutzer. It is how they are handled that needs to be considered."

"Is that right?"

"I think so," he stopped walking and looked into Amelia's eyes. "Amelia, I have the police report from San Francisco."

Amelia froze. She felt the blood drain from her face. She hadn't seen that coming and she didn't know what to say. "I didn't know that there was an actual police report."

"It was a murder."

"Yes. It makes sense, but I didn't realize ... I don't know what

I thought, but I've never seen or heard of a police report and I don't remember being questioned."

"Well, you were," he wasn't sure he believed her. "You're not the first Witch to cross paths with Scotland Yard, Mrs. Kreutzer. Do you want to tell me what's really going on?" he asked in as firm a tone as possible, when all he really wanted to do was make her feel comfortable; this lovely woman whom he wished he'd met under much different circumstances.

Her hands began to shake as she answered him, "I wish that I could … but I really don't know. I'm worried that one of those people has him."

The detective saw she was about to become unraveled. That she was telling the truth. That she really didn't know what was going on. He placed both his hands around hers and waited for her to calm down before he gently asked, "Which people?"

"I don't know who they are … but they killed my mother."

"Was it The Organization?"

"Maybe."

"Do you think they have your father's body?"

"I guess … I don't know. I have no idea actually. This is all new to me."

"I'm sorry. It's new to you?"

"That night. The night in the report. That was the last time I practiced." The detective didn't say anything. "I'm telling you the truth," she said with desperation.

"Alright then, Mrs. Kreutzer. In that case, should I be concerned for your safety?"

Amelia took a moment to answer. *Yes, you need to be concerned for my safety and it's nice that you're worried about it, but what is it that you're going to do, Detective?* she thought. Finally she said, "No. Just don't stop looking for my father okay?"

"I've not strayed from my investigation regarding your father's body, Madam. I just thought you might guide me to where I should be looking for it."

"I don't know."

"Okay."

Detective Carlisle nodded respectfully and walked away, leaving Amelia alone in the center of Trafalgar Square. He left abruptly on purpose. It was a method he'd used in the past to get people to share more with him than they intended to. Walking away with the last word generally left a person with something to say and, in turn, on their next meeting they usually overcompensated, telling the detective more than he had originally asked. He was fairly certain that it wouldn't work with Amelia. She'd had a lifetime of practice deceiving herself. It was almost second nature, but he took the chance that, in this case, hiding was something that she did not want to do.

Amelia turned around in the square. She felt lost among all the tourists and businessmen rushing by her, going about their day… their normal day … their monotonous routines that she now envied. She wanted Detective Denny Carlisle to come back, to invite her to a pub … to talk about something else, something she knew nothing about. She was fascinated by him, this ordinary man with extraordinary knowledge who'd chosen his dangerous and ever-evolving occupation, presumably because it was what he wanted to do—not because he was born into it. He knew exactly who he was and by that Amelia was both fascinated and jealous.

As she watched him disappear down a nearby street, Amelia felt lost. She was alone again. Chillingly alone and unsure of which direction she should go. Jeremy watched both of them from the front steps of the Gallery. He'd seen them walk by his office together and decided to follow at a conservative distance. He'd wanted to join them, but then thought better of it. He wondered exactly what it was they were talking about. He wondered why she hadn't told him the detective was there. And he wondered how long it was going to take Amelia to make her first mistake with the outside world, if she hadn't just done so already.

chapter 19

Dusk settled into night and a chill settled over London. The city was cold, but busy with the exception of one very quiet street. Beyond what seemed to be a small forest on Millionaire's Row, lay Jeremy's 15th Century-style mansion that, itself, sparkled like a priceless antique. It was an authentic reconstruction with all of the finest modern amenities, including a converted horse stable that housed his large collection of automobiles. The interior of the estate reflected that of a well-traveled man and also paid homage to the old ways of fine art. Deep colors of red, chocolate, forest green and spun gold wrapped around the house in pure elegance. There was not one area any less than extraordinary in the twenty-room palace.

Jeremy, Summer and Amelia were in separate rooms, cleansing in ritual baths. They were preparing for whatever the night guided them to. It was a test run on Amelia's abilities. They knew that nothing might come of it, but they were all excited about the possibilities.

Jeremy soaked in a tub of steaming water filled with herbs and sea salt. The room was lit by an endless number of candles. There was white for cleansing and indigo for insight and vision. He was focused, but tense. Lifetimes had been waited for the moment when this special young woman would embrace her unparalleled power and Jeremy was whole-heartedly convinced that

Amelia was, in fact, "The One." He was also determined to guide her and to stop anyone, or anything, that threatened to get in her way—in *their* way. In that regard Jeremy was confident. He had only one real worry—that Amelia's physical and mental state might not allow her to embrace what was coming. For him that was really what this night was about. His heart raced with anticipation as he thought of what might be ahead of them. On this night he would know. He would see Amelia's raw, unpracticed abilities, and he would know where the state of Witchcraft and "The One" stood going into the night of the Full Blood Moon.

Summer also soaked in a hot bath of sea salts and herbs. She let her hands float upward on the surface of the water. She was trying to meditate but she was shaking with nervousness. She wasn't sure Amelia was "The One." There was a part of her that wanted only that and another which hoped that she was just a girl—just Grace's daughter—a Witch with great abilities, but with no pressure to perform them; a girl who could go and try to enjoy the rest of her life.

Amelia was strangely calm and very aware of herself, noticing that all her feelings were moving forward and toward the magick within her in a very natural way. With her eyes closed, she rested in a tub that sat in the center of a bathroom which was five times the standard size. She'd lit a single indigo candle which bore an eerie glow and partially illuminated a stained-glass skylight above her. The herbs in the bath infused Amelia with memories. The tingle of the peppermint, the calming of the lavender and the womblike sensation the milk created, as it wrapped around her body, took her to the far-away consciousness of her past—to the beginnings of her lessons in Wicca and The Craft.

Amelia opened her eyes and looked down at her hands and the rest of her body as if she was seeing herself for the first time. Then she heard music. It seemed to be coming from within the room, but there was no stereo, no speakers. She thought it might be coming from the music room downstairs but it was getting louder and more clear until, finally, she recognized it. It was "Pastoral."

She sat up. *Wolfgang?*

She looked over her shoulder toward a mirror in the dressing area and found herself in what she knew was a vision, but was so real that for her it looked and felt no different than reality.

Twenty-eight-year-old Grace stood there, fastening her pentagram necklace. She turned to Amelia, who wore the same very serious and curious expression that she did so many years ago when she was bathing for the Mabon ceremony. Grace smiled and, in the next moment, it was the body of seven-year-old Amelia in the tub. Adult Amelia, was still there and very present and aware, but now within a body being controlled by her seven-year-old self.

"Is that where you hide it Mommy?" Little Amelia asked in reference to her mother's necklace, just as she had twenty years earlier.

Grace placed her hand over the pentagram. "It's not hidden. For me, the power is here," she said as she moved her hand over her heart. "The copper is one of my magickal tools that I charge with energy for rituals or protection or even just to let people know who I am when I want them to recognize me as the Witch who guides our Coven. It's a symbol of who I am and the magickal abilities that I yield and represent."

Amelia looked confused; still thinking that her mother's power somehow came from the necklace, rather than from within her.

"It is a symbol of my power, not the power itself. Once you come into your own, you won't have to search for the power Amelia, you will only need to realize it and then accept it with a pure heart and a focused mind. The only tool you truly need is you." Grace took off her necklace and laid it on the counter. "You know what to do," she said as Amelia's twenty seven-year-old body returned.

Amelia nodded, very matter-of-factly, to her mother. Then she closed her eyes and sunk back down into the tub, until she was completely submerged. Amelia was relaxed. She let the water soothe her until the peppermint on her face stirred something in her and she quickly sat up, opened her eyes and looked around; unsure if her mother had just been there or if she was dreaming.

She stood up to get out of the tub and then, with focus and clarity, she envisioned the night ahead as she dried her body and began to dress for the ritual. She hoped the night would bring back everything she'd forgotten in this life and everything that lay suppressed from the many lives she'd lived before. That was what she wanted and that was what she would request of the entities who would come to surround her.

Amelia walked over to a dressing table where the two black velvet bags that she had taken out of the chest in her office were sitting. Lying on top of one of them was the pentagram necklace that Grace had always worn in ceremony. The other bag remained closed. Amelia ran her hand over the necklace. She hadn't taken it out of the bag before she got into the bath, she was sure of that, but there it was, staring up at her, waiting for her to put it on.

chapter 20

Jeremy and Summer entered the room he'd set for the ceremony at the same time. Both of them were surprised to find Amelia already there. She had opened all the windows and was sweeping the area where the ceremony would take place with a ceremonial broom, ridding it of any old energy that might disrupt them. She was wearing a long white cotton dress, just as her mother always had during ceremonies and celebrations. She was very comfortable, at ease, as if she were in her own house and had been practicing Witchcraft her entire life. Jeremy and Summer relaxed at the sight of her, although they were both a bit taken back at her resemblance to Grace and surprised to see her wearing Grace's necklace. They'd both assumed William buried all of Grace's tools and signature jewelry along with her body.

Amelia was focused and, as usual, down to business. She began the ceremony without a word of acknowledgment. She opened the second velvet bag and removed the athame that Grace had used on the night she was murdered. As she raised it toward the north and began to walk a Circle of Protection around the three of them, Summer felt a panic rising in her chest. In a way, it was that night happening all over again for her. Jeremy squeezed her hand both to comfort her and to re-direct her focus. They needed to concentrate on Amelia, not the past, and because they had no idea where Amelia would be led. Their full attention was of the utmost importance. Summer looked to Jeremy, clearly having second thoughts about what they were doing, concerned about what Amelia would do and if she could handle it. Jeremy nodded to Summer, that everything was alright, and not to interrupt. Placing her faith in Jeremy, Summer took a deep breath and let herself go. She would allow Amelia's spirit to take her where she wished.

Jeremy and Summer closed their eyes as Amelia completed the Circle of Protection.

> *This Circle of Protection,*
> *will serve us well.*
> *To guide in all good forces.*
> *To guide away any spells.*
> *This Circle of Protection,*
> *I close on thee.*
> *No one shall break it,*
> *so mote it be.*

Amelia put the athame down and joined hands with them. She then called on the Quarters. She called the angels, Michael, Gabriel, Uriel, and Raphael, just as her mother had. They arrived quickly and she was comforted by their familiarity.

Amelia continued, the boldness in her voice rising with each verse.

> *I call on the Elements,*
> *Please forgive my past.*
> *Please aide in our doing,*
> *and help my spells cast.*
> *I stir all the Ancestors,*
> *underneath this felt moon.*
> *Your wisdom and guidance,*
> *will help heal old wounds.*
> *I summon the butterflies and the cats,*
> *come with me.*
> *I summon your magick,*

your friendship to thee.
I request the presence,
of the Winds of the north.
Your presence to guide us,
through our earth's work with force.

Amelia fell deeper and deeper into a trance as she continued. The room was very still and charged with her energy, but nothing seemed to be happening. Summer and Jeremy looked around for any evidence that Amelia was being heard. Then after a moment, the soft winds of the north began to blow through the room, butterflies filled the air and a white cat appeared. Jeremy and Summer smiled at each other and looked to Amelia, who was still entranced.

I call the Goddess Isis.
Please answer my will.
Infuse the metal of my pendant,
while I face the world.
I call Goddess Isis,
Please rise up through me.
Show me the true light,
of where we shall be.

By reciting these words, Amelia was beginning a Calling of the Goddess. It was a complicated task requiring a great deal of skill that would allow her to embody the Goddess of her choice. It wasn't something that was rare or uncommon among Witches, but more often than not it was something that was not fully completed. A Calling of the Goddess frequently filled she who performed it with an untapped energy from within, but rarely was there a ceremony in which the entity from the other world actually rose and entered the Witch's body. Summer and Jeremy were wrought with anticipation, a bit unnerved that the mighty Isis could, in moments, be inside Amelia, and equally unnerved that she might not be.

Then a presence came into the room, and into Amelia, that physically shook all of them. Amelia looked to Summer and then to Jeremy. She stared at each of them for only a few seconds, but she was looking at them intently and they could "feel" her eyes. They could "feel" her scanning their inner beings. It was as though she'd physically entered their bodies and turned them inside out.

Amelia closed her eyes and, after only a moment of complete darkness, she was catapulted into a vision. First she heard a splash. Then she saw the pentagram spinning in the water of the Japanese Tea Garden where she had dropped the rock as a child. "For every action there is a reaction," her mother's voice echoed.

Then the voice of the man who had been watching her that day replaced her mother's. "The itsy bitsy spider went up the water spout ..." As fast as it came, the voice was gone and the spinning pentagram koi pond became a clock with hands moving forward at a steady pace.

Then, again, her mother's voice echoed through Amelia's mind. "The cycle of existence, of light and dark, of glory and pain, and of life and death, is an ever-turning wheel that has no beginning and no end ..."

Amelia watched as the clock became a fountain running through the home of Isis in Ancient Egypt. Amelia saw a young boy playing on the floor with a wooden ball and within a moment the ball was a scorpion. It raised its tail and hooked it into the boy letting all of the poison it held flow into the child's veins. Amelia could do nothing but watch and, after staring at the boy, she realized who it was. Amelia was somehow within the story of *Isis and the Seven Scorpions*, as it was happening. The boy was lifeless on the floor. His lips started to turn blue and the color drained from his face. The scorpion responsible sat nearby, not boasting, but not concealing itself either. Then again, Amelia heard the man's voice from the Japanese Tea Gardens. She looked around and saw no one, but it seemed the words were coming from the direction of the scorpion. "... Down came the rain and washed the spider out ..."

A noble woman hurried into the room with Isis, Nephthys and Selket following. They surrounded the boy. They focused and began to chant, and Horus came back to life. "… *Up came the sun and dried up all the rain* …"

Amelia spun around, again trying to identify where the voice was coming from. She turned to the scorpion and in a blurred moment, she was gone.

Amelia found herself one amongst the stars as the sun and moon crossed in an eclipse and her mother's voice echoed through the solar system "… The eight-tiered wheel turns through the seasons, changing our surroundings and influencing what we do, how we feel and who we are …."

Amelia felt heat on her legs. She closed her eyes to scream with agony as it increased. When she opened them, she found herself among four other Witches in a small Scottish village. The year was 1563. They were tied to stakes and had been set aflame, just outside the church, for all the villagers to see. As the flames grew higher and hotter, the cries of the accused Witches rolled across the countryside.

Amelia's screams pounded though the rooms of Jeremy's mansion.

It was all Jeremy and Summer could do to hold on, to let her keep going, as it was now clear that it was in fact Isis who was inside of her, not in place of Amelia, but with her, showing her all that she wanted to see—showing her who she had been and where she was going.

Amelia suddenly felt cold and fresh. She could smell the earth. Then she realized she was in it. Not buried, but a part of it. She watched and felt the life force of the earth as a field of crops grew with life then died, collapsing to the ground in an instant, only to again regenerate itself again and again. She then heard her own voice and she understood what her mother had begun to say.

"Each time of the year is special, different in a way that progresses us and the ever-turning cycle of life. Always bringing change and new things. Always bringing hope for the future and wisdom from the past …"

From the soil of the field to the dust of another town square, Amelia found herself in a man's body surrounded by people shouting at her, pointing fingers and accusing so many things so loudly that she couldn't understand any of them.

Then she felt it. It was a stone hitting her, then another and another. She was in the town square of Salem, Massachusetts. It was the year 1692 and she was reliving yet another one of her lives, and deaths, as a condemned Witch. Again she screamed and gasped for breath. Summer and Jeremy, both wanted to stop, to pull her out of wherever she was, but they knew they couldn't.

A rock smashed into Amelia's temple and everything went black for what seemed like an eternity. She finally opened her minds eye and watched as an eagle soared high above the earth, beautiful and majestic ... seemingly at peace. She had been this eagle. She watched it glide, then look down on its prey and dive. "... and, if we allow it ..." her mother's voice said as if it were brought by the wind, "The cycle of existence will bring with it the higher purpose of our lives."

Amelia flashed on an Indian village. It was not from her past, but something that existed in the present. She watched as three accused Witches, an elderly woman, a man and a young girl, all killed themselves in the middle of their village, to avoid further torture or a painful death by the hands of their accusers. Amelia scrambled. This was not from the past. This was something that she remembered from her current life. A story she'd seen on the BBC recently, but now she was there, watching it happen. It was a modern day fear of the unknown manifesting and the self-inflicted injustice that followed.

Then, from a voice in her memory, Amelia heard what Jeremy had said to her and realized that the other night was not the first time she'd heard him speak the words, "All beings are inherently magick, it only need be realized ..."

Amelia was then in her grandparents home. She walked toward Jeremy, who was with her seven-year-old self.

Little Amelia sat on Jeremy's lap where he appeared to be reading her a story. He whispered in her ear while her father talked on the phone in the next room. "All beings are inherently magick, it only need be realized. For most it will never be known. For some it will come more naturally than for others ..."

Amelia had no time to react to the fact that Jeremy was speaking to her about Witchcraft against her father's will. She was now back in the Japanese Tea Gardens on the afternoon her mother died, watching herself with her mother.

"The One?" Grace asked.

"Yes, Mommy. Who is she?"

"Nobody knows."

Amelia moved in close to her mother's ear and looked around to make sure they were alone. She winked at her adult self and then whispered, "But, I know Mommy."

"You know what?"

"I know who I am," she said. "She's growing inside of me."

Grace's eyes went wide as young Amelia's smile stretched out across her face and the glimmer in her eyes became so bright that they seemed to glow.

The glow became so bright that the adult Amelia had to close her eyes. When she opened them she had returned to being a voyeur, watching her seven-year-old self with Jeremy as he continued to talk to her about Witchcraft. He was holding up a storybook to mask the conversation so that William wouldn't notice and Amelia would learn unconsciously. Jeremy turned from little Amelia, as if to look directly at adult Amelia, and into her vision. Black smoke came out of his mouth when he spoke and his appearance became somewhat distorted. "... and for a select few, the magick within them can not be ignored."

Amelia's body shuddered at the image, but the vision remained. Jeremy's eyes lingered on her as the black smoke continued to pour from his mouth. Then the voice of the man who had watched her in the tea gardens was back again to complete her favorite nursery rhyme with his daunting tone, "And the itsy, bitsy spider crawled up the spout again."

What felt like a bolt of electricity shot through Amelia and the vision ended abruptly. She'd sensed that something wasn't right in the room. The Goddess Isis stayed with her as her eyes popped open. Then, in one swift moment, the cat sat down, the butter-flies landed and remained still, the candles went out and her face whipped over her shoulder toward a wall where there were three long open windows.

In an instant, Amelia slammed all the windows shut with her sheer will. Jeremy and Summer turned. First they saw nothing, then in the darkness, they saw them; the men of The Organization fleeing. One man remained in the shadows, his eyes locked with Amelia's. He was frozen by her stare, as if he were prey mesmerized by a hunter. She finally released him, he ran toward the others and Isis was gone from her.

They all watched as the men pulled away in their black sedans. Then they turned to each other.

"How did you know?" Jeremy asked Amelia.

"I just did," she said, lying down on the floor in the middle of the Circle, physically drained.

Summer looked her over as if she was now someone else. "What made you decide to perform the Call of the Goddess?"

"I didn't decide. It's just what was intended … at that moment."

Jeremy was amazed, which was a rarity. Amelia had never remembered him being impressed with anything—with art, yes—but with people, never. This was different. He was almost giddy. "Even though you didn't practice, it continued to evolve within you. This is going to change everything. I know that Samhain will bring something extraordinary."

Amelia stretched, now sore from the experience. "Maybe we should move the Goya opening to the weekend following Samhain," she said, now that she was beginning to understand what she would be dealing with and why so many people wanted control of her.

Jeremy shook his head. "It's much too late for that. And it's perfect. You'll be surrounded by security and a crowd up until we leave to perform the ceremony."

"He's right," Summer agreed.

"But that's not when I'll need security. And no one can really protect me, can they?" Amelia looked to both of them. "My body will be weak when the power is coming into me, like it is now, won't it? Even more so, I'm sure. Until it's all in me, I'm vulnerable. The only protection that I'll have until sunset the following evening is the Circle and the two of you, right?" Summer and Jeremy didn't know what to say, but it didn't matter. Amelia received her answer in their silence. She knew that the only person who had a chance at protecting her was herself. "Well, then," she said. "I'd like to release the Corners, close The Circle and go to bed."

chapter 21

October 28, Three Days to the Full Blood Moon

The early morning fog began to lift and London came to life as Amelia sat in the graveyard, writing a letter to Wolfgang. She was having her morning scone and coffee at his headstone, just as casually as if they were having breakfast together at home. Mr. Paskin watched her from a distance, as he had so many times before, but that morning he noticed something different about Amelia. He couldn't figure out what it was, but there was something distinct and new about the young woman. It was in the way she carried herself. Her sorrow was still there, but it was obvious that something new in her life had given her hope, or a new outlook. She seemed better. He was happy to see it in her, and thought she might be taking a positive turn in life until he realized that she was writing another letter.

Sweetest Wolfgang,

I wanted to write you last night after everything happened, but my body was exhausted and my mind was still swirling with energy. I could not calm myself enough to put my experience into words and I don't think I would have had the strength to hold a pen. It was all I could do to get to sleep. What I uncovered within myself last night was extraordi-

nary. I was shown history that I'd never known, given insight into things that I would have otherwise overlooked, and I actually experienced some of my past lives. It wasn't just that I saw them. I felt them. I was there. It was only moments, but I was there and Isis was with me. She was guiding me and it was amazing because I know that nothing happened to my body physically, but it's as if my physical self didn't exist. I was like air. And the most wonderful thing was that I felt my mother. As much as you remember someone after they're gone, there is a sense of them that you lose. Her spirit was with me again. I'd forgotten part of her after so many years. Not who she was, but the feeling of her, emotionally. I don't ever want to forget that part of you. I'll never let you go. I promise.

It wasn't just an awareness of my mother and my past that I got last night. I was so conscious of everything that it's hard to describe. My senses were attuned to the everyday things. The little things. My sight. My hearing. My touch and sense of smell were all so strong that my awareness, as a person, showed me far more than what most humans will ever know about the world. I experienced the details of all the living things around me, not just the single perspective of my human life.

There was also a darkness in the world that became more clear. Not as clear as the goodness, but I could see secrets and I could see lies. I only wish I understood them and what they meant. In the darkness, I also realized my extraordinary desire for revenge for the life I've been robbed of, for the people who have lost their lives because of me. For you. I know those feelings go against all the laws of Wicca and The Craft, and I know I should tell someone how strong they were and still are, but I don't think I can. I can't impose that kind of fear on Jeremy and Summer and I can't bear their reaction. It wouldn't be fair.

And with Jeremy, there was something last night, something dark within him. Black smoke came from his mouth with all of his words, but I couldn't figure out why. There is a secret that I'm sure he's keeping, but at the same time I feel he has a protection for me that is unworldly. He is a contradiction that I do not yet understand and I can not entirely trust him. So again, that is why, my darling, the only one I can turn to is you. I know that once you hear me you will guide me. I miss your hugs and kisses. Come and visit my dreams soon.

All of my love,
Your wife, Amelia

Mr. Paskin watched while Amelia folded the letter, that she'd so carefully written on fine parchment, and sealed the envelope. She then proceeded to dig a hole in the earth next to Wolfgang's headstone and bury the letter. She covered the mess she made of the earth with sunflowers, as she had been doing for the past three years. Then she got up and left for The National Gallery, having no idea, that once again, Mr. Paskin was watching her.

It wasn't something that he was necessarily in the habit of doing, but he did worry about the girl and ever since a heavy rain had uncovered all of Amelia's letters the winter before Mr. Paskin had known. He had known, but he hadn't told a soul. Not even Amelia. Not even his wife. He'd cleaned up the mess before anyone had noticed it. He counted almost a hundred letters, then he tied them together, put them in a bag and buried them right back in the earth under Wolfgang's headstone. From then on Mr. Paskin attended to the maintenance of the gravesite personally. He wanted to be sure that none of the letters came up through the earth again. He was terribly concerned about how Amelia might react if they did and if she was the one who found them. He didn't want to know what would happen if she realized that, beyond the world she had created for her husband in her mind, all she had done was bury letters in the dirt that would never be read.

chapter 22

Detective Carlisle began his morning at Caffè Nero and took his time getting into the office. He knew the day would be a quiet one so he'd decided to enjoy it and move at his leisure. He was a man who understood that there was a time to push a person and a time to wait. He would no longer be digging through the life of Amelia Pivens Kreutzer. Now he would wait for her to come to him and in the meantime he decided it might be a good idea to brush up on his knowledge of Witchcraft and hopefully learn something new.

The interesting thing about Detective Carlisle was that he believed. He believed in the practice and he believed in the magick. He'd actually seen some Craft magick, first-hand, in his life's travels and he in no way doubted the power of a true Witch. What he did not yet know, however, what the detective had not yet uncovered, was one of Witchcraft's oldest and deepest secrets. A secret that they'd buried right in front of his eyes and the eyes of anyone who cared to see. Detective Carlisle had not yet read or come to understand the truth behind the legend of "The One," which the ancestors had so skillfully hidden in the form of a children's book that anyone could buy at virtually any metaphysical shop in the world, and many mainstream book stores.

When he finally reached the office, *The One: A Fairy Tale of the Ancient Witches* was sitting on Detective Carlisle's desk among a number of other books and magazines on The Craft. There were somewhere around forty and the piles covered his entire work area.

"Judith," he called out in a reserved but curious tone.

"Yes," his young and eager new secretary said, appearing at his door immediately.

"What is all this?"

"Everything on The Craft I could find."

"Oh."

"You said *everything.*"

"Yes. I did. Thank you. Where did you get all this?"

"Mysteries, some used book stores and the museum store."

"The museum store?"

"At The National Gallery. I thought, since there are a lot of Witchcraft-related images in art, maybe they would have something, and they did. I also picked up the information on the new Goya Exhibit that's coming. It looks amazing."

"That it does. Thank you Judith."

"Of course."

Judith left and the detective, using the best of his skills, decided which book to delve into first. He closed his eyes and picked one. He opened his eyes to *London Witches Falling Down: An Unofficial History of The Organization.* He contemplated the title, wondering what would prompt someone to write such a book. "Well, I suppose I've got to begin somewhere," he said to himself, easing back into his chair with his coffee perched just right as he settled in for an afternoon of reading.

chapter 23

When Amelia arrived at the office, she found she was still too consumed with the events of the night before to focus on her work. She tried. She attended to the guest list for the Goya Opening and signed the everyday paperwork that had piled up in her in-box. She even put a call into Diana at Chanel, a woman who she'd come to know through her late grandmother, and asked that she choose an elegant, but simple black gown that she could wear to the opening. She made a list of all the many things she needed to do, but it wasn't long before Amelia found herself standing before the Isis trunk. She swung the door to her office closed, opened the lid and removed her mother's Book of Shadows.

It was a large leather-bound book with copper-covered wrought-iron clasps and it was over five inches thick. Amelia had seen it many times before, but she had never given much thought to the symbol on the cover. It was a Briar Rose—the same Celtic design she'd bought at Mysteries. *Odd,* she thought. *I guess my subconscious was working on that purchase.*

She opened the book and on the inside cover looked at where her mother's magickal name was listed. "Ireland" was what she called herself. Amelia never quite understood why her mother had chosen that name or why she even had one. On more than one occasion Grace had asked Amelia to choose a magickal name, explaining that it would be used in ceremonies, the recording of their practice and all things involving The Craft. Amelia's answer had always been the same. "My name is Amelia and that's magickal enough for me,"—an answer that Grace adored, but knew would change some day. She let her daughter win the battle to use her own name as a child because she knew that as an adult it would be easy for Amelia to understand the importance of it. She would take one if for no other reason than to protect her true identity.

Amelia looked at the cover of the book, then she took the Briar Rose charm out of the paper bag that was still in her purse. She unclasped the chain that held her wedding band and slipped on the charm so they hung right next to each other. "Briar Rose" would be her magickal name she decided and, without putting a second thought to it, she put her necklace back on and picked up a pen to begin her writing.

Amelia flipped through the book, through her mother's spells, recipes, potions, drawings and ritual details. She noticed, as she had before, that her mother had ripped a number of pages out of the book.

She wondered what was on those pages, but casually dismissed their absence. She was sure that Grace had removed them for good reason and that was enough for her. Amelia loved knowing that she was the only other person on the planet to have seen the contents of the book and that, when she died, it would be buried with her.

The privacy of the Book of Shadows was something about The Craft that Amelia liked and respected very much. It was considered a diary of sorts that no one would see but she who wrote in it, unless specific instructions were left to pass it on to a relative. On the inside cover, under the name "Ireland," Grace had written a statement declaring that the book was not to be burned or buried upon her passing, as was tradition, but given to her daughter.

Amelia reached a blank page and ran her hand over it. It felt good, special, like being the first to make tracks in fresh snow. She began to write and the words flowed through her at a furious pace. She wrote down every detail of the previous night from the ritual bath to the fact that she was almost too excited to sleep when she finally made it to bed after the ceremony. She described how she slept the deepest sleep that she'd experienced in years after she finally calmed down. She wrote until her hand hurt, until she'd written everything there was to write.

Then she finally felt released from the night before; ready to move forward and direct her attention to her paying job and the Goya exhibit, which was only three days away from opening. Amelia closed her eyes, closed the book, and then placed her hands over it.

> *In the realm of magick,*
> *this book shall reside.*
> *No one but the chosen,*
> *shall see what's inside.*
> *For those of the nature truly can see.*
> *That this is my will,*
> *so mote it be.*

She got up to put the book away and there was a knock at the door. "Just a moment."

Claude opened the door and peeked his head in just in time to see Amelia hiding the book in the Isis trunk. He thought nothing of it until he saw the look on her face which immediately revealed that she was hiding something.

"I'm sorry," he said, worried that he'd upset her.

Amelia had a delayed response. No one had ever known where she kept her mother's hidden treasures, or even that she had them— but then again, it was only Claude. She decided that he probably thought nothing of it. "No worry. What's new today?"

"Many things, Madam. But isn't the real question, 'What's arrived today?'"

Her face lit up. "What's here?!"

* * *

Jeremy, Martel, Claude and Amelia all stood before *The Sickness of Reason.* Claude looked to Amelia, who closely examined the faces of each person portrayed in the drawing. "It's a satire on members of society who impose rules on others but have no intention, themselves, of following them. They did, however, use these rules as a tool to judge others."

Claude looked to Martel for his reaction to Amelia's review of the painting.

Martel took the cue and added, "Goya once said, 'The world is a masquerade. Face, dress and voice, all are false. All wish to appear what they are not, all deceive and nobody knows anybody.'"

Amelia considered the quote and turned to Jeremy to regard him in terms of Goya's words. She loved him, but she knew that there was a side of Jeremy Roth that was probably nothing like it seemed to be.

Jeremy could feel her examining him. "Nobody wants to know what's *really* going on in the world because we all have some secret aspect of ourselves that we don't want others to know. Isn't that right Amelia?"

She only raised her eyebrows in response. Claude and Martel could not help but notice the silent tension between Jeremy and Amelia.

"It's all personal choice and perception, when commenting on the world," Martel said, "and Francisco Goya, he was truely one of a kind."

Amelia turned to Jeremy. "Yes. He certainly was, wasn't he?"

chapter 24

Amelia invited Summer to spend the afternoon at the Gallery, but she declined. She'd decided to spend a quiet day reading by the fire. She wanted to absorb her surroundings, her current situation and the coming of the Full Blood Moon. She felt it was important not only to focus on Wicca and The Craft, but to explore the *other* Amelia—the young woman who had a wonderful life with many accomplishments for which she'd worked very hard. And, because Francisco Goya's work had such a profound affect on her, Summer wanted to know more about the artist.

She was curled up drinking tea and turning the pages of one of the many art books that Amelia had given her to look through. Summer was comfortable in Amelia's house and she loved being snuggled under a blanket inside while the world outside was so terribly cold.

The sitting room was quiet and still. She stretched her arms and rearranged herself on the couch for a short nap, completely unaware of a man from The Organization, who was inside the house and watching her from the next room. Summer closed her eyes and only a few minutes later, she heard the floor creak.

She opened her eyes and looked around, but saw nothing. *It's just the house adjusting to the seasons,* she told herself as the man moved closer to her.

Summer no sooner closed her eyes again before she heard another creak. She sat up this time, scanning the room carefully. Still, there was nothing, but she got up anyway.

She sensed something moving closer to her. She quickly drew a Circle of Protection around herself with her finger and marked the boundaries with a few white candles from the nearby coffee table.

> *With this Circle of Protection,*
> *I create.*
> *I will enhance my power,*
> *deliver all enemies their fate.*

She closed her eyes, working swiftly and with focus. As she continued, her words became more and more forceful and strong.

> *I stand here,*
> *under the magick light.*
> *Empower my body,*
> *with the power to fight.*
> *Protection from harm,*
> *is what I ask.*
> *Please accept this as your task.*

The man had made his way to Summer and now stood in plain view. He was only a few feet away, but was very aware of her strength. He watched carefully, waiting for a moment to attack her; wary of the Circle and where the edge was. Summer's eyes remained closed, but she could feel the man—she knew precisely where he was.

> *Come my Dragons.*
> *Come strong and true.*
> *Send me your power,*
> *send me to you.*

Lend your veil of protection,
to cover me.
This is my will,
so mote it be.

The man from The Organization lifted his foot to move inside the Circle, toward Summer, and as he did the quick, sharp snap of a bone cracking filled the air, followed by another along with the man's screams. His ankle and knee were both broken straight across and hanging unnaturallly. He balanced on one foot, holding his injured leg with only the strength of his hip, while he screamed for mercy.

Summer stood quietly, protected by the Circle, but still nervous about how close he was and what was happening and why. Her heart was pounding. She was terrified, but successful at hiding it—she appeared confident and fearless. And, more importantly, she knew that she was in control of the situation and would be for as long as was necessary.

"You'll have to do much better than that if you want a chance of getting near Amelia," she said calmly, her voice penetrating like a sharp, cold blade through the man's head.

He and Summer stared into each other's eyes. He was in terrible pain, horrified and deathly quiet. All the blood had drained from his face and he was pale from shock. Summer looked down to his hanging limb. She knew that if he lost his balance and hit the floor, the pain would be so excruciating that he would surely pass out. She was surprised that he hadn't already. The Organization had prepared him for this, she decided, to her horror, but it hadn't worked.

Now, she could see every bit of his fear. His eyes were glued to her, perhaps more because he was afraid to look at his own injury. The man quietly withered in his private hell as he did what he'd been trained to do—wait. He knew that there was help coming. He knew that they were right outside the door, watching. And he knew they were waiting to see if Summer stepped outside the Circle, either to help him or to run. If she made herself vulnerable, then they would go after her first and save him later. That was procedure. But this man saw the look in Summer's eyes and knew that he and his partners had no chance.

After almost ten minutes, the man was dripping with sweat and close to falling. Summer remained in the Circle, watching him, when she heard the front door open followed by the sound of feet running across the hardwood floors. Two men in solid black suits came into the room, picked up the injured man, and then left.

As soon as they were out of sight, Summer sat down in the Circle, wrapped her arms around her knees, and started to cry and shake with fear. They were coming for her, to scare her, or maybe to kill her. She didn't know their exact intentions, but she knew they wouldn't stop. They would keep coming until they got whatever they wanted. That was why her spell of protection broke the man's bones rather than just throwing him back away from her.

Summer knew, from that moment, that Amelia would be constantly watched, examined, and maybe even "taken" so that this rogue group, hiding within The Organization, would be the first to try and control her and "The Ultimate Power" when the Full Blood Moon came closest to the earth on Samhain. They couldn't risk Amelia being in complete control of herself and they would not underestimate the strength of the opposing Witches who, they were certain, had a plan to kill her before sunset on the First of November.

Summer knew that the countdown had begun. Now, anything standing in the way of these men would be eliminated. She only hoped she could hold them off long enough to get Amelia to that night—the night when they would not only face The Organization, but when the Civil War of the Witches would finally come to a conclusion.

chapter 25

As the day came to an end, Martel and Amelia found themselves leaving The National Gallery offices at the same time. They
decided to walk out together, taking the long way and wandering
through the Goya exhibit on their way out.

Martel stopped in front of *The Family of the Infante Don Luis
de Burbon,* a royal family portrait by Goya and one in which the
artist had painted himself. *"Sobre cada fabla se entiende otra coas."*

Amelia smiled. She did love Martel's intellect. "To every story
there belongs another," she said, quickly making the translation,
which impressed Martel to no end. "Werner Hoffman, quoting
Juan Ruiz, whose quote is rather fitting for all of Goya's work ...
and for all of us for that matter."

"Us?"

"The human race."

"The cruel world," he joked.

"Not cruel. Real."

"Really?" Martal said, smiling.

"Okay, cruel *and* real."

Martel laughed.

"What?" she said.

"You."

"Me what?"

"Do you always say exactly what comes into your head the moment the thought arrives?"

"I try to. Is that wrong?"

"No. It's refreshing."

"Well, I'm happy to have refreshed you, then."

Martel and Amelia made their way down the front steps of the Gallery and through the car park, both of them enjoying the tingle of the cold air.

"It's all a bit cynical," Martel said. "This outlook you have on the cruel and real world."

"It's not just my outlook and I didn't say there was anything wrong with it. Conflict is the most interesting part of life."

"Is it?"

"I think so," Amelia laughed.

Then, out of nowhere, a distrubing chill come over her and Amelia's mood turned. Suddenly, she found herself wanting nothing more than to get into her car and drive away, but she didn't know why.

Martel didn't notice. "You're a bit mad, aren't you?" he said, as they walked by a man of The Organization. The man was doing nothing to conceal himself. He was just standing there, watching.

"A bit," Amelia said, handing Martel her bag. "Excuse me, for just a moment," she said, and turned to walk toward the man.

"Amelia?" Martel called out, confused and rather uncomfortable. He held his breath as Amelia approached the stranger.

"Hello," she said, leveling her stare on the man, who said nothing in return. "Visiting?"

He remained silent.

"Because I know you don't work here and this is staff parking only," she said, stepping closer. Now she was right in his face— they were literally nose to nose.

Martel was stressed. He didn't know if he should get help, or step in. He had no idea what Amelia was doing or if she even knew this man.

"Mrs. Kreutzer," he called out.

Amelia didn't answer. She ran her eyes up and down the man, remaining very calm and cool. "So … are you hunting me? Or just watching?"

The man didn't move.

She smiled, looking into his dead eyes. "Right. I'll see you later then. Tell your friends I say, 'Hello.'"

She walked back to Martel to find that his smile and warm manner had gone cold.

"What's this?" he asked with narrow eyes and reserved frustration.

"Nothing."

"Do you *know* that man?"

"We just met, actually."

Amelia and Martel continued to walk through the car park. "How is the case going with your father?" he asked.

"They haven't found anything," she responded, somewhat surprised and a little offended by the question.

"I'm sorry."

"Thank you."

"It's rather odd."

Amelia looked to him quizzically.

"A body being stolen for no reason in particular. It's odd."

"Yes. Yes it is," she agreed, surprised to find herself responding to such a brazen comment.

"In all of my travels I've never heard of such an incident."

"Yes. Well, I suppose I haven't either. There are a number of very disturbed people in the world and London is certainly no exception."

Just then another man from The Organization appeared. He made no attempt to hide. He stood there, watching, just as the other man had done.

Martel was now very uncomfortable. He saw that Amelia noticed the man and did nothing. Martel stopped walking and confronted her. He'd moved past being apprehensive and was now extraordinarily angry. "Are you having security problems here?"

"No."

"We are only days away from the opening."

"I realize that," Amelia replied.

Martel glanced at the man who remained standing in the shadows of the car park, watching them.

"I know there is a situation with your father and for that I am truly sorry. But if you are concealing a personal or professional problem—if something that you're doing places my *paintings* in danger—then, not only will I pull every piece that you have on loan in an instant, but I will contact all the other museums with which you deal and see to it that The National Gallery is never loaned another piece of art for as long as you're in it," he said trying to contain his anger. "Do you understand me, Mrs. Kreutzer?"

Amelia was shaken by his sudden shift in demeanor but her reply was equally fierce and direct. "Yes, I understand. And I assure you, Señor Demingo, that none of *The Prado's* paintings are in any danger, nor is The National Gallery. Good Night."

Amelia got in her car and closed the door. She looked around—someone had been inside. She could sense it, but she couldn't determine what was different. Slowly and carefully, she turned the key and Beethoven's "Pastoral," performed by Wolfgang, blasted from the stereo speakers at the highest level of volume.

Amelia sat back in her seat trying to decide if she was more scared or angry at this violation. Someone had put the CD in her car. Someone had broken into her car to do this. *For what?* she wondered. *Just to make me mad?* She stared at the CD player, then hit eject. She examined the CD carefully. It had a drawing of Isis on it, but nothing else.

She looked at her rearview mirror and saw that the man was still watching her. *So you boys know what I'm up to. Okay.*

She put the CD in her purse and wrapped her hands tightly around the steering wheel. She knew that this was The Organization trying to break her, just as Summer and Jeremy had warned.

Well, it looks like you win round one. Amelia looked in her rear view mirror to see the man still watching her as he got into his black sedan. She was too distracted to notice that Martel was watching both of them from his car.

Amelia threw her car in reverse. It was time to let out a little aggression. She hit the gas and peeled out of the car park in a rage. "Care to join me?" she said, looking back to make sure that the man was behind her, hoping that he would follow, no matter where she went and what she did. When she reached the first stop light, Amelia took one last conspicuous look at the man. Then, before the signal turned green, she hit the gas, showing what her BMW Roadster could really do. "Let's play," she cackled like a demon as the adrenaline pumped through her body and her car gained speed.

Amelia tore through the streets of London like a maniac, daring the man to keep up with her, while she played cat and mouse with the fog, the red lights, and the endless roundabouts. The risk made her feel good. Being close to death, now, made her feel more alive than she'd felt in years. She did not want to die that night, but she was enjoying herself, giving no thought to the fact that with one wrong move, both she and the man behind her could be in the following day's obituaries.

He stayed on her tail all the way home. Then, he simply slowed down, turned around, and drove off in another direction.

Amelia watched him go. *Ah, well then. What could be waiting for me behind door number two?* She turned the corner to find another black town car parked outside her flat. *What a surprise.*

Rather than pulling in to park, Amelia stopped in the middle of the street. She took a heavy flashlight out of the glove box and walked over to the car. She knocked on the passenger side window. The man inside remained motionless.

She turned the flashlight and shined it on him.

"Hello." Still nothing. Now she moved the flashlight, looking around the car. On the passenger seat she saw an open file folder, full of documents and, next to it, a stack of photographs. She looked closer and realized that the files and photographs were all about her, Summer, and Jeremy. The photos were recent—all taken over the past few days. Amelia raised the flashlight, as if to knock again, and then surprised the man by shattering the window instead.

Without flinching, the man started the car. Amelia reached in to grab the file, but got only one page before the man drove away.

She stood in the street, watching him go, until the black town car rounded the corner and disappeared into the night.

Summer watched from a second-story window of the flat. However, she was not only watching Amelia. Summer also had her eyes on Martel, who was hiding in the shadows and watching Amelia from his parked car.

And, unbeknownst to Summer, Detective Carlisle was also there, in an unmarked car just down the street, watching all of them. He'd had a hunch that there would be something for him to see at Amelia's flat and he'd arrived just in time.

Amelia parked her car, folded the paper and put it in her purse. This was an incident that Summer and Jeremy didn't need to know about. She knew that neither of them would approve of what she'd done and she didn't want the lecture that she knew would come with it, so she let the moment go and started toward the front door.

chapter 26

Walking up the front stairs of her flat, Amelia smelled boldo, a Chilean plant that instantly flooded her with memories. Boldo was her mother's favorite tea and she hadn't smelled it since the day she died. Grace had been drinking it in the park that afternoon. Now, ground leaves from the plant were scattered all around the outside of her house. Assuming it had to do with a spell of some kind, Amelia carefully opened the front door.

She found the front room filled with purple, black and white candles that led up the stairs and back into the kitchen. Purple represented power and religion, black was for banishing negativity, and the white was for protection and doubled as a symbol of the moon. Beyond the candles was the smell of an over-powering incense. Amelia walked into the kitchen to find the makings of it on the counter. She ran her hands through the basil, sage, frankincense, myrrh and pine, concerned by what exactly had prompted the appearance of these ingredients.

"Hi," Summer said, coming up right behind Amelia and unintentionally startling her. "I'm sorry. I didn't mean to scare you."

"It's okay. What is all this? What happened?"

"They came for me."

Amelia took in Summer's words. "The Organization?"

Summer nodded. "I should have known. I should have been more prepared."

"I'm sorry."

"It's okay. It's not your fault and now I'm ready for them."

"But it is my fault. They came because if you're out of the way, it's easier for them to gain control over me, right?"

"That may be why they came, but they're going to have to try a lot harder if they think they're going to get me away from you. They can't do it Amelia. Not while we have each other."

Amelia was uneasy about Summer's role in what was happening. This responsibility was becoming too much for her and Summer could feel her apprehension.

"I'm going to teach you, Amelia. Jeremy and I are going to stay with you and teach you everything that you need to know. Once we've prepared you, these men won't have a chance."

"You don't know that for sure."

"No, but it's something I believe and you should too."

As much as she appreciated Summer's concern, Amelia decided that this had gone much too far. She couldn't be responsible for placing yet another person's life in jeopardy. She just wouldn't do it. If The Organization or the opposing Witches wanted her ... well, that was fine; but it would be only *her* that they took. She couldn't live with someone else dying on her behalf. "I can't be responsible for you, Summer. You should go home. I'm sorry. I just ..." she hesitated. "I need you to leave."

Summer placed her hands over Amelia's to stop her from continuing. "Amelia, this is inevitable. It doesn't matter *where* I am. The fact of the matter is that this is exactly where I'm supposed to be. This is my purpose in this life. It's not just personal for me. As much as I'm here for you, Grace's little girl, I'm also here for the future of Wicca and The Craft and myself. This is what my entire life has been about."

Amelia looked into Summer's eyes and knew that she wasn't going anywhere. No matter how out of control and dangerous the situation became, Summer would stay by her side. She would die there if need be and that was something that would not change. It was admirable and although it wasn't just about her, it still made Amelia uncomfortable.

"I don't know what to say, Summer."

"Don't say anything. Focus on resting tonight," she said with a positive force. "The Blood Moon is coming quickly and so is the biggest night of your career."

"This is very serious. This is all very serious."

"And it always has been. It's just that you're realizing it for the first time and it's a lot to take in. I've always known. There is nothing that can be prevented or changed now. All we can do is wait for the moon ... and you. So, I propose that you take tonight to sleep and that we change the subject for the remainder of our evening. It's important not to forget the rest of your life. Everything you do plays a part in everything that happens to you. It's all connected."

"I understand," Amelia said, having no choice but to go along with her.

"Good. So, how is the exhibit?"

"It's coming along. All of the paintings aren't quite in the right place yet, but I'm confident I'll figure out what to do at the very last minute."

"But, for now, you're playing musical artwork?"

"Basically. We always do this. No matter how much we plan and prepare where to hang each piece in advance we inevitably change it all at the very last minute."

"And how is Señor Demingo? Has Romeo asked you to be his date for the Goya opening, yet?" she asked, unconcerned with the answer, but hoping to gain some more insight into this man whose motives she was so unsure of.

"His opinion of me has changed. The crush is definitely gone."

"Oh?"

"He can tell there is something going on with me and he knows about my father's body. He thinks it's something to do with the museum—that I might be involved with something that could put *The Prado's* paintings in danger. He's requested a special meeting with security."

Maybe that was why. Summer contemplated. *It is millions of dollars worth of art that The National Gallery has on loan and Amelia and Jeremy are essentially responsible for it. Even though Jeremy is as cool as they come in any given situation, Amelia isn't. And to a man such as Martel, the assumption could easily be that the tension between Amelia and Jeremy has something to do with their upcoming event; that there is the possibility of something going wrong. My God.* Summer thought. *If that's why Martel is following her, then what does he think is going on? A security risk? The threat of a robbery? And if that isn't it, who in the hell is he and what is he doing here? What does he want with Amelia?*

"Are you okay?" Amelia said to Summer, whose eyes had glazed over as she pondered Martel's possible motivations.

"Yes. Fine … a little tired I guess."

"Well, there's nothing I can do about it."

"What?" Summer asked, having lost her train of thought.

"Martel's paranoia about security. I can't tell him anything."

"No. Of course not."

"He'd pack up his paintings and leave. Then he'd see to it that I was fired and I'd never work again."

"Absolutely. You're going to have to finesse your way through it with him."

"I'm trying," Amelia stretched her arms up over her head. "I've got to go to bed."

"Good idea. You should get some rest."

"I'm sure going to try."

Summer watched Amelia walk up the stairs. She wasn't tired at all. Her mind was racing. She decided to stay up and make a list of what they would need for Samhain.

* * *

Once she was in her bedroom, Amelia found herself uncomfortable and in no mood to sleep. Summer could hear the wood creaking as she paced the floor. Amelia was raised as an only child by a single parent and lived most of her life by proper British rules. She was was accustomed to being alone and not responsible for anyone else. Wolfgang had been the only exception, but now there was Summer and Amelia couldn't bear the thought of anything happening to this woman. She had traveled so far and watched over her as though Amelia were her own daughter. She knew that Summer had come for Grace and that was why Amelia wished she would go home. Summer had endured her best friend bleeding to death in her arms and now, because of Amelia, it was possible she'd be faced with that same kind of horror all over again.

Amelia closed her eyes and took a deep breath. She needed comfort and she needed sleep. She stopped pacing and rolled her wedding band through her fingers. Her eyes welled with tears. *Take me away.* She opened one of her dresser drawers that was filled with Wolfgang's possessions: his favorite shirt; the sweater he wore around the house on his day off; the platinum ring she'd given him on the anniversary of the first time they met; and his cologne. She picked up the bottle and opened it, letting herself get lost in the memory of his scent. She took it to her bed and put a dab on the pillow. She got under the covers and grabbed another pillow to wrap her arms around. Then Amelia closed her eyes to fall asleep with her husband. She knew it was an unhealthy vice, but she didn't care. It was something she hadn't done in quite some time and she knew it would assure her a full night of rest, which was exactly what she needed.

chapter 27

October 29, Two Days to the Full Blood Moon

Amelia and Claude stood before Goya's *Dreams of Lying and Inconstancy*, a drawing of a woman with two faces, positioned between her two lovers and a two-faced servant girl covering for the women. "Both women are involved in triangles of deceit and lies—one by cheating and the other by protecting her employer's deception," Amelia explained as the image drew her in. Again, she had the feeling that the intent behind Goya's work was winding around the reality of her life like a hungry boa constrictor.

"Is this a reflection of something Goya experienced personally?"

"Maybe, but I think he did this one because he was trying to comment on what we consider scandalous behavior. What he's presented here is, by definition, scandalous. But it is also typical of the human condition, whether we act on it or just think it."

"And for you?"

"For me, the drawing represents truth bombarded by rules created by the people who break them. Deception is deception, whether it's followed by a physical action or not, in my opinion," she said.

"I see. No one is completely faithful to anyone, but themselves ... He really couldn't help but look at things for exactly as what they were, could he?"

"No," Amelia agreed, "he couldn't." She drifted off. *Because no one is faithful. Not one species. There is always competition and so being faithful isn't really natural. The combination of all life in the universe, working as one whole, is all that can be trusted. That's why The All is the highest recognized power of The Craft, not the God or the Goddess.*

"It's a wonder he didn't die of madness," Claude said, disrupting her thought.

"What?" she snapped back into the moment and turned from the drawing to Claude. "I mean, yes. It is a wonder that he didn't die of madness isn't it?"

"Or perhaps he did."

"Perhaps ... so, Claude," she said, wanting to change the subject so her thoughts of The Craft wouldn't take her over in front of him, "opening night is right around the corner."

"Don't worry about a thing, Madam. My team is fully prepared."

"I'm actually not the one who is worried this time."

"Oh, yes. Señor Demingo is meeting with my staff over tea this afternoon."

"Ahh ... Very good. Have you seen him today?"

"Not yet."

* * *

Martel took a tuxedo from a man behind the counter of a small tailor shop on Charles Street in Mayfair. "Thank you, Sir."

"It's my pleasure, Señor Demingo," the tailor said. "It's nice to see you again. Please give my best to your mother."

"I will. Good afternoon."

"Good afternoon."

The men made significant eye contact as they shook hands and their identical copper rings brushed each other.

Martel walked out the door and pulled on a pair of gloves which covered the ring so, by the time Summer spotted him, it was concealed. However, he didn't see Summer. She made sure of that. She was not there by coincidence. She'd decided that following him was the only way she could determine who Martel was and whether or not he posed a threat to Amelia. She was across the street, hiding in her car, spying on him. She'd been following him since he left his hotel that morning.

Martel got in his car and pulled away. Then Summer pulled out, following him at a safe distance.

chapter 28

As Detective Carlisle sat in his office and turned the page of *Witchcraft & Wicca Magazine* to continue reading an article on the coming Full Blood Moon, Amelia turned the page of her Goya event schedule for The National Gallery staff. She scanned her list, reading the main points out loud, "7:00 p.m. Security ready at their posts; 7:30 p.m. Coat Check Opens; 7:30 p.m. Bar Opens; 8:00 p.m. Doors Open; 8:30 p.m. *Quinta del Isis* Introduction … *Isis* … damn it."

Amelia was frustrated. She wanted to concentrate, but she was too distracted even to read what was directly in front of her. It was *Quinta del Sordo* not *Quinta del Isis*. She wanted to do what was expected of her as a born Witch, but at the same time, Amelia did not want to sacrifice everything she'd worked for. She wanted to enjoy her big night and she certainly deserved it, but it didn't seem possible. How could she when she was too preoccupied to even review a simple list?

Amelia opened her purse and took out the CD that The Organization had left in her car as well as the page she'd taken from the man whose window she'd smashed. She scanned the document. It was a chronology of her life and the sanitary, factual manner in which it was presented disgusted her.

1. *Born October 31, 1977.*

2. *Mabon 1984. Witnessed mother's murder. Summoned virtually the entire magickal universe to try and save her mother. Broke all rules of The Craft, subjecting herself to face, someday, The Law of Three.*

3. *October 1984. Moved to London.*

4. *February 1985. Introduced to Jeremy Roth.*

Amelia stopped cold on:

5. *October 31, 2003. Amelia's 25th birthday. Wolfgang Kreutzer, husband, eliminated.*

Amelia stopped reading. She lingered on the word "eliminated." She didn't look at the rest of the list. What it said didn't matter. Not now. This meant it was true. Summer and Jeremy were right. It wasn't the record of an accident that she'd hoped for. The Organization had taken Wolfgang's life. They had in fact *eliminated* him and, as far as Amelia was concerned, that was entirely her fault.

So which one of you black-suited bastards did it? Her body tensed. *That's what I'd like to know. Because, if I have to do it with my own bare hands, I'm going to watch you die . . .* Amelia noticed that her hands were clenched so tight that her fingernails were digging into her skin. *Jesus Christ. I can't do this right now.* Amelia put the page and the CD back in her purse. *I can't have these kinds of thoughts.*

* * *

Amelia wandered through the Goya exhibit, taking in her favorite artist. She was trying to escape her world and consume herself with his, if only for a little while. She stopped before *The Clothed Maja* and stared into her eyes, wondering who the woman in the painting really was and considering how different *The Clothed* and *Naked Majas* really were. Yes, it was the same woman in the same pose, and on the surface it simply seemed that one was clothed and one nude, but that idea was too simple. She knew they were two halves to one whole, but was one of them more dominant? Was one the representation of the woman's true self and the other the façade of what society expected her to be? What was hidden within her smile and what, of it, did Goya know? Did he even care or was she simply a tool for making another artistic comment? A comment that belonged solely to him and in which he wasn't actually portraying the woman, but himself? Why, Amelia wondered, did it feel so incomplete and almost inappropriate to have hung *The Clothed Maja* before her naked sister had arrived?

Amelia rolled her wedding band through her fingers. As much as she could distract herself with questions, it would still be one of those days when she longed to be with her husband. She couldn't get the page she'd taken from The Organization out of her head. The word "eliminated" consumed her. It was bad enough that she'd awakened this morning, forgetting that Wolfgang wasn't in bed beside her. She knew that was her own fault. The cologne always got her to sleep but it always haunted her the next morning.

Jeremy recognized her mood as he walked toward Amelia. He knew the look, the stance, the sorrow of which she wouldn't speak but that surrounded her enough for even strangers to notice. He'd seen her this way many times, but it had been quite a long while since it was this intense.

"How are you holding up?" Jeremy said as he approached her and *The Clothed Maja*.

Amelia didn't answer with words—only a sorrowful expression on her face—as she turned her bright eyes on his, shooting her pain right through him. Amelia had a look that could break even the coldest man's heart and this was it.

"We'll get through this," Jeremy said.

"Why couldn't you just let me believe it was an accident? That it wasn't my fault?"

"It wasn't your fault."

"But it was because of me."

"I'm sorry that we told you, but please don't think of it as something that happened just because of you. There is a way of life and a belief system that you embody and it is not something you choose. It's too big for you to feel responsible for everything it causes to happen."

"So, now I'm Joan of Arc?" she said, more in sadness and disappointment, than anger.

"Oh, Amelia, don't."

"My mother knew and so did my father, but Wolfgang had no idea. He knew nothing of The Craft or of my past other than the fact that someone murdered my mother. He was completely innocent … they shouldn't have hurt him."

"Can I take you somewhere? For a walk? We can go for a nice lunch."

"We've never been busier," Amelia said, becoming more emotional and frustrated. "All of the paintings aren't even here yet and the ones we've hung need to be moved. The placement plan isn't working. It doesn't feel right. This is my favorite part and I can't even do it. I can't concentrate on anything."

"And that's because you're trying to concentrate on everything. We can take a few hours off and start fresh this afternoon."

Wanting anything but to spend the afternoon talking about how she felt or what was expected of her on the night of the Full Blood Moon, Amelia lied. "I have so many errands to run … so many things for the opening, and for myself. I'm just … I just …" She threw her arms up in the air. "I'm at the end of my rope."

"We'll make a list and I'll send someone out for you."

"No. It's easier if I go and actually, I want to go. I want to be alone. If you could help with placing the paintings then I could go."

"Of course."

"I miss him today, Jeremy."

"I know you do."

Jeremy knew she was lying about her errands, but it didn't matter. He wanted to ease her pain in any way she needed, although he did wonder how she really planned to spend the afternoon. He was concerned that, in her emotional state, she might do something without thinking it through first. But, whatever it was, he'd have to step back and let her do it.

"What?" she asked, watching the wheels in his head spin.

"I'm trying to figure out how to get a smile out of you."

Amelia shook her head. "That's not going to happen. Not today. I have tough days and this is one of them. There's no way around it. You know that."

"What if we traded cars?"

Amelia couldn't help, but smile. "Which one are we talking about?"

* * *

Amelia pulled out of The National Gallery car park in Jeremy's Aston Martin V12 Vanquish while, inside the museum, Jeremy stood before *The Clothed Maja*, trying to determine what Amelia was so engrossed in when he found her.

"She's missing her other half," Claude said, as he stopped to watch his boss contemplate the painting. "She's incomplete without *The Naked Maja* hanging next to her. Each one needs the other for them to make sense, to each other."

Jeremy again contemplated what Amelia might have been thinking as she stood before the painting. *Does Amelia feel that she is incomplete without her other half? I wonder. Does she need the descendant of the opposing twin, in order to feel like a whole woman ... or a whole Witch?*

Jeremy looked from the painting to Claude and considered his observation.

Detective Carlisle picked up the children's fairy tale of *The One* from his stack of books on Witchcraft.

At the same moment, Amelia pulled over and opened her mother's address book to the page listing the address of The Organization.

chapter 29

Summer watched from her car as Martel walked into a hotel. Through the sitting room window, she could see that he was meeting with a well-dressed, proper Englishman in his 40's. The men exchanged a few words, then the man handed Martel a letter and left.

Martel stayed and ordered tea. A few moments later Claude and a number of National Gallery security guards joined him.

The well-dressed man, who'd left Martel, walked down the front steps of the hotel and down the street toward Summer. She was too engrossed in watching Martel to notice, but as the man walked by her, she felt his energy and looked up. He stared into her eyes, letting her know that he'd been aware of her presence since he arrived. He wanted her to know that and he wanted her to see him up close, so there would be no mistake about who he was. As he flashed an arrogant smile, Summer's body went numb, paralyzed by fear. She hadn't realized who it was in the distance. She'd parked too far away to identify him during his meeting with Martel, but as he passed her by, Summer sat frozen and unable to react. She now understood that Amelia's situation was escalating, as was hers. This was a man who Summer knew and who Summer feared. This man, with whom Martel had spent the past hour, was a world-renowned practitioner of black magick. His name was Dorian Caldwell.

chapter 30

Amelia sat in Jeremy's car listening to the CD that The Organization had left for her. As the music continued she realized that it wasn't just Wolfgang playing "Pastoral." It was a recording of his very last performance. *How did they record this?* She was baffled. The track sounded much too clear to be a bootleg, but there had been no recording there that night. Wolfgang would have said something to her. He would have been there planning. She would have remembered.

Amelia looked at the massive building she'd parked in front of; it was an old structure that appeared to be a museum. It seemed to be looking right back at her. *Who are you people?*

The Organization's chronology of her life was on the passenger seat, along with her mother's address book. Amelia picked up the page and scanned it, somewhat fascinated by the time-line of her life as it was recorded by a group of fanatical men whom she'd never met, or even seen before the past few days.

"Amelia Pivens. Scorpio," she read aloud, "with Leo rising under the Chinese year of the Snake. Well, you know who you're dealing with, guys, don't you?" she said and looked back to the building. "So, I guess you know how pissed off I am just about now."

Amelia continued reading. She skipped to the bottom of the page where someone had begun a note regarding the Calling of the Goddess she'd performed at Jeremy's house.

*Although the ceremony was successful and extraordinarily pow-
erful for someone who has been away from The Craft for so
long, there is a hate and revenge in her soul that will make
her easier to manipulate once she comes into her full power.*

Amelia folded the page, put it in her pocket and got out of the
car. *Let's see how easy I am to manipulate today.* A number of surveillance cameras followed as she walked toward the entrance. With
so many lenses, it was as though a hundred sets of eyes were following her as Amelia approached the front door, but there was
only one man in the surveillance room, waiting patiently. That
man was Dorian Caldwell and the building that Amelia was approaching was The Organization.

chapter 31

Jeremy closed his office door and logged onto his computer. He clicked "Favorites" and went to his personal "Aston Martin Security Site." He then clicked a button that read "Vehicle Tracking Device" and typed in "Locate Vehicle." Within seconds, a map of the world appeared and the program began searching. The map shrank to Europe, then England, then London, then the district of Mayfair.

Over the changing images there was a flashing red box that read "Locating Vehicle." When the flashing stopped, "Vehicle Found" appeared in its place, in green lettering. Jeremy sat back in his chair as the address of The Organization came across the screen.

"This is one that I wish I'd been wrong about, child … Why couldn't you just leave it alone?"

Jeremy unconsciously balled his hands into fists and his body tensed. For the first time he was concerned, stressed. The Organization was predictable for the most part, but Amelia had imposed herself on their territory. It was an act that was just not carried out by a Witch, or any woman for that matter. Jeremy wasn't even sure a female had ever set foot on the premises—not one who'd left with her life intact, anyway.

Jeremy had been afraid that Amelia was going to do something she shouldn't that afternoon and he'd only hoped that it wasn't this. The thing he dreaded most was that she would go to The Organization. However, he was not at all surprised that she did.

"Why?" He took a deep breath, asking himself a question that he already had the answer to. He knew her logic—that was the point of him spending his life with her. Amelia was not one to back down. She had no fear when facing an enemy and, in most cases, she invited it.

This was a trait that empowered her, allowing her to overcome whatever the obstacle was. It had worked positively for her throughout her life, but in the case of dealing with The Organization, Amelia couldn't have been more wrong in her actions. And because of her emotionally-driven state, Jeremy's mind exploded with thoughts about the many things she might be doing there; things that would make their already volatile situation worse. He wondered what she might be doing to provoke The Organization to take her or kill her even sooner than they had planned to.

chapter 32

Summer stayed with Martel, even after her encounter with Dorian. She knew who Dorian was, but Martel was someone she still needed to understand. She couldn't just assume he was a part of the rogue group within The Organization. She had to consider the fact that he may have had no idea who Dorian really was. Many of the men in The Organization had power and wealth. Their members included those who were connoisseurs of the finer things in life, fine art included. That could easily have been the reason for Dorian's meeting with Señor Martel Demingo, or the pretense for it anyway. Dorian could have presented himself as someone willing to make a donation to *The Prado*, The National Gallery or any number of things. It wouldn't have surprised Summer at all if The Organization had a Goya of their own and were inviting Martel to view or or borrow it. They would pursue any avenue that would provide more access to Amelia's world and inner circle.

When his lengthy meeting with security ended, Martel stayed at the hotel and relaxed with one more cup of tea. Summer watched as he used his moment alone to review the notes he'd spent the afternoon taking. When he did finally leave, she followed at a conservative distance. She was sure that Martel was not aware of her, but very concerned that Dorian had known exactly where she was. She was desperate to know the connection between them.

Martel pulled into The National Gallery car park at half-past four. Summer stayed a safe distance behind him, but also pulled in and parked. She looked at her watch as he walked into the building and decided to leave. Her fears were shifting more toward Dorian by the minute. It was possible that Martel posed no threat at all; that he was just in the middle of a situation that he knew nothing about. However, Summer was sure that Dorian had involved himself with Martel for a reason and whatever that reason was, it was dangerous. She needed to know what it was.

Summer reversed the car to go home and meditate on what Dorian's tactic might be. She was about to drive away when Martel, Jeremy and Claude walked out together, deep in conversation. She watched as they all nodded. It was clearly a very serious matter they were discussing. *About security.* Summer presumed. *Or maybe Martel mentioned to them that he'd met with Mr. Caldwell that afternon and Jeremy was explaining the risks involved in dealing with The Organization—without revealing his own allegiance to The Craft.* Whatever it was, Martel looked distressed. He got in his car and drove away, and Summer decided to follow.

chapter 33

Amelia was led through the halls of The Organization by a well-groomed man in a solid black suit. He was silent as they wound through the imposing gothic structure. The building was so quiet and empty she wondered for a moment, if they were the only two people in it.

Amelia examined her surroundings carefully. The artwork of dark legends and the torture of accused Witches decorated the walls and the building itself looked, and felt, like an ancient prison from which one could not escape. The chill that ran through its cavernous halls quickly made its way to Amelia's skin and into her bones.

Amelia followed the man into a large office, where two men were waiting for her. The younger of the two stood up and extended his hand, "Dorian Caldwell."

Amelia did not respond. She stood almost motionless. Angry.

"Sit please," he said, a bit surprised that this was how she chose to start a meeting with him, in his place of business, to which she had come unannounced.

Amelia sat down and looked Dorian over. In his element, he was clearly a holier-than-thou man of unworldly smugness and demented morals. He sat down behind a large desk and folded one hand over the other. Amelia's eyes traveled up from him to a painting of Pope Innocent VIII hanging behind him. "Do you like it?" Dorian asked. "It's an original."

"I'm sure it is," she said coldly, recognizing the man in the painting as the Pope responsible for the deaths of thousands of Witches.

"This is my associate, Francis Brunning," Dorian said, gesturing toward a distinguished older man, sitting so quietly in the chair next to Amelia that she hadn't even noticed him.

"Hello Amelia."

She sensed a familiarity in his voice, but she couldn't place it. "So, you *do* know me?"

Dorian smiled. "Of course. Is that why you've come? To see if it was real? This life you've ended up in?"

"No. I've come because I have a request—two requests, actually." Amelia got up and placed the paper on the desk in front of Dorian. "I realize you intend to destroy me in one way or another, but before you do, I'd like to give my father a proper burial. You understand. After all, you are good Christians, right?"

Dorian looked to Francis. Then, after a long moment of silence, the man who had led Amelia to the office returned. "Mr. Brunning," he said, "You have a call."

"Thank you. Excuse me, Mrs. Kreutzer," he said getting up.

Amelia turned back to Dorian and his sinful, prodding gaze.

* * *

Martel had a mobile phone to his ear. He was sitting in his car, parked just outside the gates of The Organization. Not far down the block and across the street, Summer was watching him closely. She couldn't believe he was there, but she had to consider that, he too was, there, spying—perhaps on a man with whom he was considering doing business. Perhaps with a man Jeremy Roth had just warned him about.

Martel glanced at Summer through his rearview mirror as he continued his telephone conversation. "She either followed me or she was already here … No. I'm sure she doesn't realize I see her."

* * *

Dorian looked from Amelia to the page she'd stolen. "You do understand that this is not a list of orders. It is simply a standard field report which, incidentally, does not belong to you."

"Well, thank you. I'm much more relaxed now."

"And, as for your request, I have no knowledge of your father's body or its whereabouts."

"I somehow don't believe you."

Dorian smiled, "I can't take credit for something I didn't do Mrs. Kreutzer. That would be wrong."

Dorian's arrogance annoyed Amelia. It was pushing her over the edge. She wanted to fight with him and rather than discourage her, he led her right into the lion's den.

"We are not in the business of robbing the graves of unimportant men, Mrs. Kreutzer. Our purpose is only to stop the evil that is plaguing our earth and the institution of organized religion."

"I don't believe those are truly your motives, Mr. Caldwell, but if they are, what is it exactly that makes Witches the chosen evil?"

"We did not choose. You did. We follow God's wishes. You take the power of the world into your own hands, with complete disregard of how it affects the lives of others."

"We believe that all faith is good as long as it's positive. If a persons' belief makes life and the universe better, then, we believe, the chosen God is their choice. How can it be evil or even wrong to allow a person his or her own choice?"

Dorian smiled and answered her with a glare. This infuriated Amelia even more.

"Tell me," she continued, "Is it our celebration of the earth that you believe is evil? Is it the practice that you should give back to life and the world all that you take from it? Is it the acceptance of all people, no matter their race or gender? Is it that we consider all life equal? Or is it the promotion of the betterment of oneself, through oneself, rather than existing to take orders from a group like The Organization, that you and your friends oppose, Mr. Caldwell?"

Dorian didn't miss a beat. He laughed at her. "Those are the rules of Wicca my dear, not all Witches. But if the rules of Wicca are, in fact, what you say, and if they are the standards you're holding me to then, that is fine. I positively believe in my mission for The Organization and I believe that, by what I am do-

ing, I am helping all humans move toward a better world. Therefore, I think my beliefs satisfy your little rule, don't they, Amelia?"

Amelia leaned over the desk until she was only inches from
Dorian. He was bigger, but she was close enough to snap his neck
and mad enough to do it. "Can you really claim allegiance to this
organization of devils you have here, when you are breaking their
rules and deceiving, even them, for your own purposes?"

"Touché! Good show, darling."

"So young, for a woman of such power," Francis said. He'd
returned just in time for their face-off. "We don't want to fight
you, my dear—only conquer you."

Amelia turned to Francis. "Power comes from the passion with
which you believe. It is not for you to decide what is right and
wrong. As you say, it is for the individual. The passions that fuel
one's belief are what makes them real and that is why, in this world,
the possibilities are endless."

"You are the man I am here to see," Amelia said, suddenly
realizing that, although Dorian's passion filled the room, it was
Francis who was *his* superior.

He nodded.

Amelia found something about him strangely familiar, but
she couldn't place it. "We've met before."

"That is an experience that, I believe, I would remember. Now,
Little Amelia, what can we do for you?"

"D.H. Lawrence taught that in the unconscious mind of every human being there is a dark God lurking and that it is just a
matter of wanting to open that door."

Francis raised an eyebrow.

"You want me to open that door, don't you Mr. Brunning?"

Francis was curious to see where she was going, but not the
least bit intimidated by her brass. He was actually rather pleased
by it. "The doors you open are your choice, alone, Amelia ... and,
it seems, you have already come to a decision about which ones
they will be ... You had a second request. What is it?"

"I want to know who was responsible for the death of my
husband. Who exactly?"

Francis didn't answer her, but Amelia saw the answer in his eyes, literally. She found herself hypnotized by his stare and, through the reflection in his eyes, she remembered. She remembered the big black town car screeching around the corner, all the confusion on the street, the people turning and running, the man driving the car who didn't appear to be at all out of control. He was wearing a solid black suit. He was a man of The Organization ... Amelia blinked and when her eyes opened, back to Francis, she was even more spellbound. She saw the car coming toward them, then a man pulling her out of the way. It was a man who had been at the concert. It was Dorian Caldwell ... and, as he pulled Amelia out of the way, he kicked Wolfgang directly into the car's path.

The images stopped and Amelia shuddered.

"You will burn in hell, Mr. Caldwell," Amelia said without turning to him, without taking her eyes off of Francis Brunning, whom she then addressed. "You do understand that, because of what you've done, I don't value my own life enough to serve you, just so I can live."

"It's not that we won't eventually eliminate you, Amelia. It's just that there's something we want, before we do."

"You will not win this battle Mr. Brunning. I am everything you believe me to be and more."

Her statement amused Dorian. "Like a kamikaze pilot, I gather? Intriguing."

Angry, but confident, Amelia walked out of the room, down the hall and out the front door.

Both men watched her leave from the window.

Summer gasped when she saw Amelia storm out of The Organization and get in Jeremy's car. "Amelia! Oh, my God! What are you doing?" She started to jump out of the car but then thought better of it.

Dorian couldn't take his eyes off her. He was like a hungry wolf, licking his lips. "I hope she's right. I hope she is everything we believe her to be, and more."

"She is," Francis replied, with confidence.

"I know she is," Dorian cackled. "It runs in the family."

In the safety of the car, Amelia let her guard down. She was terrified. She pulled out of the driveway and onto the street. Half-a-block away, she stopped the car and began vomiting. She didn't want this. She couldn't handle it and she didn't want to be any part of the coming Full Moon. She wanted to die—right then and there. She wanted to lie down in the cold earth, next to her husband, and leave her life behind.

The perimeter security cameras from The Organization followed Amelia closely as she wiped the vomit from her mouth with her shaking hand. Francis was watching her carefully, as was Detective Carlisle, who was parked directly across the street from her.

"There we go," Francis said, while he enjoyed his tea in a room filled with security monitors.

> *The itsy bitsy spider,*
> *crawled up the water spout.*
> *Down came the rain and*
> *washed the spider out.*
> *Up came the sun and*
> *dried up all the rain.*
> *And the itsy bitsy spider,*
> *crawled up the spout again.*

Amelia sensed something. She hadn't heard Francis, but she sensed him and what he was doing. She turned back toward The Organization and, unknowingly, looked directly into one of their security cameras, right at Francis. He sipped his tea. "One more day, luv. One more day."

Summer sat in her car, watching Amelia, still in shock that she had actually gone to The Organization. She pressed a ringing phone to her ear.

"Jeremy Roth," he answered.

"It's Summer. We need to have a talk with her tonight."

"I know."

Francis leaned back in his chair, still watching as Amelia pulled away. "Goodnight little one." He turned to another monitor and watched Summer pull out in the same direction. "Goodnight Mother Earth." Then he waved to the security camera in which Martel appeared as he drove off. And, finally, Francis turned his gaze on the illustrious Detective Carlisle, who had been there the whole time watching all of them, well-aware that he was being watched right back.

"Oh Detective. Detective Denny Carlisle," he raised his tea cup as if to toast him. "Always a pleasure."

The detective stared at the security camera. He knew where they all were and he wanted to be seen. He wanted The Organization to know that if anything were to happen to Amelia Pivens, he'd be coming after them.

Francis smiled, "Everybody loves a good party I suppose. My goodness, Samhain should prove rather exciting with such wonderful guests." He laughed.

chapter 34

When Amelia finally went home that night she found Summer and Jeremy waiting for her.

"Now they know," Jeremy said with an anger that reduced Amelia to a childlike state. "They know what makes you tick, your vulnerabilities. You've given them exactly what they wanted."

"I still can't believe they let you in the building," Summer said, as she paced the floor.

"Of course they let her in. Just think of how much information they got? And she brought it right to them, all wrapped up, like a present with a bow. Good God, Amelia! What were you thinking?"

Amelia took quite some time to say anything. There was so much running through her head that she couldn't put it together fast enough to speak and she didn't want to. She could hardly breathe. She needed a moment and she would take it. She hated being torn between herself and her new and overwhelming obligation to The Craft. She was a grown woman who'd just had the rug pulled out from under her in life. Now, she was being scolded for acting on behalf of herself instead of the greater good of a practice that she respected, but had not chosen. She had never asked for the life she was living. She also resented the fact that Jeremy could have her cowering over her actions; second guessing her and doubting her own good judgment.

She looked up at him, green eyes shining through the jet black hair that she let cover half her face, and said, "I don't care."

"I beg your pardon?" He straightened up and looked at her as if she'd just slapped him across the face.

"I don't care if I've given them exactly what they wanted and I'm beginning to wonder why the two of you care so much."

"Amelia, we ..." Summer tried to jump in, but Amelia raised her hand quickly to cut her off.

"Don't. Just don't. And don't try and play mother innocent. I want to know why in the hell you were following me?"

"Well, you *should* care," Jeremy said, stuck in the preceding moment.

"Well, I don't!" Amelia shouted. "We've covered that and moved on, Jeremy, and I've asked a question. And the next one is, why were you tracking me?" she demanded, making it more an attack than a question. "Here Amelia, take my car. Relax. Enjoy the day ..." she said, mocking him. "Fuck you, Jeremy."

"Twice now, in the past few weeks, I've heard vulgarity out of you that I've not heard in the entirety of your life," he said, trying to hide the tremendous pain her words caused him.

"My entire life has been rather different than the past few weeks, don't you agree?"

"You need to care about the circumstances you're in, Amelia," Jeremy said, not about to let her gain control. "You've got to fight this battle with intellect and reservation, not rage. There's too much at stake. You're putting the lives of other people in danger out of your own selfishness and vengeful thoughts—all because these people took your husband."

"You're damn right! All because these people took my husband ... and my father ...and my mother ... and now they want me. You're absolutely right, Jeremy. I do have vengeful thoughts. I'm sorry. Were you expecting something else?"

"There is an age-old war going on here."

"That's not my fault."

"No, it's not, but this is a very real situation. It's as if you don't understand that. I don't know what you were thinking going there?"

"I WANTED TO KNOW!" she screamed.

"YOU WANTED TO KNOW WHAT?!" he shouted back at her, slamming his hands down on the table in front of him. He scared the hell out of Summer, but Amelia didn't move and he stared right into her eyes. "What did you want to know?"

She didn't answer.

"What Amelia?!" He wasn't about to back off and was more frustrated with her by the second. "Sometimes, I look at you and all I see is your mother and her mistakes, all over again. You've invited them into your life now, just as she did. It's not personal Amelia. This isn't just about you! This is precisely the kind of recklessness that got your mother killed."

"What are you talking about?"

Jeremy didn't answer her. He looked away, having said more than he wanted to. Amelia turned to Summer. "She invited them into her life how?"

Summer's approach was just the opposite of Jeremy's, as was her tone. She was careful and almost soft in her manner. "All of us are at risk now, Amelia, and we need to be mindful of each other. We've reached a point where we must think things through. Quick or irrational reactions could get us all killed and jeopardize the future of The Craft. That's what happened with your mother. She opened herself up for more than she could take on."

Amelia stepped back. Her shoulders dropped. Summer had her attention and, in one moment, she was a child again; willing to listen to anything that Summer had to say.

"There are two significant battles going on within this situation and you are at the center of both of them. I know you resent that, but you can't change it. The All chose you to bring this power to the world, so that you could give The Craft a second chance. So that you could undo what was done by the High Priest Domhall and the High Priestess Maeve so long ago, and so that you could bring a power to the Witches that would see The Organization to its end.

"The power is your responsibility and you must use it wisely. You must find closure in how Wolfgang died, without hurting anyone in the process and then you must let go of him, once and for all. He will always live in your heart, but you must accept that he is gone from your life, Amelia. Wolfgang is dead."

"I know that," she said, like an angry child with her face buried in her hands.

"Good," Summer said, unaffected by Amelia's tone. "It's October and there is no better month to give yourself over to the moon and the universe; to let them guide you toward separating your past from the purpose of your future. Jeremy is right. There are thousands, millions, of Witches who will be affected by this. I know this was not your choice, but you are all that The Craft embodies.

"Your place is no longer in the life you created, but in the greater universe. At least for the present—until we know for sure whether or not you are 'The One.' We are only two days away and where you are, as a Witch, is remarkable. But your state of mind and your personal turmoil could place you in an unbalanced situation when the moon is closest to the earth. This must stop or you're going to create a vulnerability that we can't afford, Amelia.

"If you don't work with forces that are positive and pure, you will have no walls to protect you. You will also be more apt to misuse your abilities. Your feelings of revenge could manifest themselves and there is no telling what could happen if you can't control your rage or direct your magick right away. You'll be physically weak in the beginning and this could take some getting used to. If you make the mistake of letting your emotions, rather than your intuition, guide you, and you are 'The One,' you won't be the only Witch who suffers for it.

"You will suffer the Law of Three, but for every action that you take and every desire that you feel, whether you act on it or not, there will be a reaction that will ripple and affect all Witches. The only thoughts and feelings that you can bring to Samhain are your desires for balance and harmony throughout the universe, which ultimately will make those who hurt Wolfgang pay for what they did, times three ... Please, Amelia. Take tomorrow off. Make peace with yourself and say goodbye to your husband or moving forward in this world will only be one dangerous obstacle after another, for you."

Amelia didn't say anything, but she was listening. She didn't like what she was hearing, but Jeremy and Summer could see that everything Summer was saying was getting through to her. She knew she would have to let go of the anger she'd been carrying and adding to for the past twenty years and she knew the time was now.

"Magick is dangerous, Amelia. It's powerful and it's dangerous. You must be able to control it. If your personal thoughts of anger or revenge come into the process, you will infect the magick of the most powerful moment in modern history and we could be faced with a mayhem that we could not begin to comprehend. This is why most Witches follow Wicca—for guidance toward balance. I know you know the ways, and if you just let yourself remember, they will guide you. And remember to be careful, because, even if you are 'The One,' you are still human and we don't want to lose you."

When Summer finished, Amelia was still bent over with her face in her hands and the room was silent. Jeremy and Summer sat down. The next move was Amelia's and they would give her time. They would wait for her. She was so still it was nerve racking, but also a relief because it was clear she wouldn't fight them, not any more.

Finally, Amelia looked up at Summer and Jeremy and then burst into tears. "I can try to let go …" her voice screeched with heartfelt pain, "but hanging on to Wolfgang is the only reason I've been able to get this far."

chapter 35

October 30, One Day Until the Full Blood Moon

The sun made a few unsuccessful attempts to fight the morning rain during Mr. Paskin's drive to the cemetery. It was early and frightfully cold—not a time for anyone to be visiting loved ones. He was taken back to find Amelia, under an umbrella, writing another letter to Wolfgang. He assumed she'd followed the groundskeeper in before he closed the gate behind him. It was just seven o'clock and they never opened before eight. Not without a special request.

He parked his car and waited for Amelia to bury her latest letter and clean the dirt off of her hands. Then he walked over to her.

"You're here early, Mrs. Kreutzer. Is everything alright?"

"Yes," she answered, without looking up at him. "There's just been so much going on that I haven't been over to visit in a few days. I hope you don't mind my sneaking in early."

"Of course not, luv. Anytime."

"Thank you," she replied, looking up at him, knowing that he would react to her face, but unwilling to hide from the world that day. Her eyes were swollen and bloodshot and her skin was sickly translucent. Her coloring, or lack thereof, magnified the fact that she'd been losing weight by the day since her father's body had disappeared. But what struck Mr. Paskin so profoundly, wasn't just her physical appearance. Amelia exuded a feeling of fear and hurt, of which she didn't appear to be in control. This was a woman on the edge of madness, as Mr. Paskin saw it. This was a woman who had given up—who felt she had nothing left and who, therefore, was capable of anything.

He said nothing, but without a second thought he hugged her. Sometimes, he believed, all a distraught person needs is a human touch—the love and compassion of another, without words. He held on for as long as she let him. Then, without a word between them, she pulled back and turned away. He watched her walk to her car and drive off into the city.

* * *

Mr. Paskin stood before Wolfgang's headstone. In all the years he'd been doing his job, Mr. Richard Jacob Paskin had never once betrayed a client's trust, pried when he shouldn't have, or jeopardized the feelings of a family with unnecessary details. However, Amelia had affected him that morning and it was something he was not able to dismiss —not with her feeling so alone … not with her father's body still missing.

Going against all the values he held so dear, Mr. Paskin dug up Amelia's letter. After reading only the first few sentences, he knew that he would have to call Scotland Yard. He'd ask Detective Denny Carlisle to come over quietly, but quickly.

Dear Wolfgang,

I have something very important and difficult to say. Because of the sudden shift of events in my life, I need to make a change. I need to exist only within myself, not as Amelia Pivens Kreutzer, but as the Witch—the being into whom I was born. I'm sorry that I never told you my history, but ever since The Craft killed my mother, it has been of no interest to me. I didn't think it mattered, but now I find myself surrounded by danger because of it. Now, I am faced with the men who took my mother's life, my father's and my dear sweet Wolfgang, yours.

My father's body is still missing and, with this Full Blood Moon that is coming, there are many Witches who are in danger—many people, both good and bad. When the sun sets on the First of November, the life of the modern Witch will have been changed forever and, if something goes wrong, a great deal of blood could be shed. Blood that includes my own.

I must do what I can to make what is wrong right and to bring balance back into this aspect of the universe.

Because of all this, I need to release my personal attachments. I hope that you will forgive my absence. Please, don't forget that I will be with you again, someday. I'll miss you. I already do. I don't know that I will be able to do what is expected of me, but I've got to try. I know you'll understand. I've got to let Summer guide me, so that I can do what is right. I've got to say goodbye.

I love you forever,
You wife,
Amelia.

Detective Carlisle lowered the letter and looked at Mr. Paskin. "Are there others?"

"Yes, but ..." Mr. Paskin hesitated, having just betrayed Amelia once, and not wanting to do it again.

"I don't care to read them, Sir—not yet. I only want to understand who I'm dealing with."

"She's been writing him ever since he died."

"Three years?"

Mr. Paskin nodded. "She's scared."

"I know."

"She's just a girl."

"But a strong and stubborn girl."

"Her father's body ..." Mr. Paskin gestured to the letter. "She seems to have an idea of where it might be."

"Yes. Thank you for calling. May I borrow this?" he asked, regarding the letter.

"Yes, Sir. Of course ..." he trailed off, wanting to say something more, but holding back. Unsure of the right words to use.

"What is it, Mr. Paskin?"

"It wasn't just that she was scared. She was almost ... someone else."

"How do you mean?"

"I mean ... dangerous," he said, taking a deep breath, realizing what he'd just said to a police detective, even though it was true. "It took a lot for her to write that letter, Detective—something big. She's been carrying on this love affair with her husband ever since she lost him. She bought the plot next to his, for herself, the day we put him in the ground. She brings a picnic out at least once a week and she never said good bye to him. She's been determined to keep him alive, one way or another, until this morning."

"I understand," the detective said, knowing—knowing that a woman, pushed as far as Amelia had been pushed, could be completely consumed by life, but, at the same time, have no regard for it, whatsoever—not for her own or for those around her. "Good day, Mr. Paskin."

"Good day, Sir."

chapter 36

Amelia got to bed early that night, but lay there wide awake. She'd spent the day alone. After leaving Wolfgang's grave, she'd jumped on a red bus and spent the whole day lost in the city and its people. Jeremy and Summer let her be. They'd known, from the beginning, that Samhain would bring what it was meant to bring. There was nothing they could do but advise her, wait, and be there for her. And they knew that they'd reached the point where the best way to support her was to leave her alone, so she could take some time to realize what her life could be. It was a wise move on their behalf, as that is exactly what she did. She unplugged herself from her life and took in the world as it came to her. It was the best day she'd had since her father died, but she was tired when it was over.

Amelia tried to will herself to sleep, but she couldn't. She was thinking of the letter she'd written to Wolfgang and wondering if she could really let him go. She finally got up and opened the drawer full of his things. She put her hands in, touching everything that was his. Then she stood up and looked at herself in the mirror above the dresser. She was drawn into the reflection, seeing a change about to happen in herself. Slowly, she removed the chain on which her wedding band and the briar rose were hanging. She kissed the ring and placed it in the drawer. She swallowed her tears and closed the drawer.

Then she opened a second drawer in which a black velvet bag sat amongst her clothes. She removed the bag and placed it on the dresser in front of her. She looked back up at the mirror, at her bare neck. She had not taken the wedding ring from the chain around her neck since she'd put it on three years earlier. She knew that this was a change she had to try to make; that her life might depend on it. She opened the velvet bag, removed her mother's pentagram necklace, and put it on. Amelia looked at herself ... it was as if she was looking at a different person, another woman being released from within her. She was, for the first time, making a full attempt to embrace herself as the blessed and magickal Witch that she was.

Amelia got back in bed and placed her hand over the pentagram. "I know you've moved on to the next life and I can't ask you back to this one ... but if there was ever a time I needed you to guide me, Mom, it's now," Amelia said and closed her eyes.

Outside her bedroom window, on a ledge out of her sight, blue and yellow candles burned under a bowl filled with honeysuckle, lilac and oil. The smoke from it came in through her window as she finally drifted off to sleep.

Identical blue and yellow candles burned in the center of a ritual circle at The Organization. A bowl within the circle held blue, white and black feathers—promoting change, union, and protection—and an aquamarine stone for psychic awareness. Honeysuckle and lilac surrounded the bowl in order to allow the men hidden access to Amelia's unconscious dreams.

Amelia was comfortable in her sleep. She was dreaming. The smoke from the burning oil blew directly through a small crack in her window as Dorian guided it from The Organization's magick circle. He, and the other men, were with her, in spirit, as Amelia dreamt of the night her mother was killed.

She remembered opening her eyes to the fairy and seeing shadows coming upon The Coven from all directions. Then she remembered the shadow of the killer and the knife, raised high in the air, plunging down at her mother. She relived the moment when Grace's body fell to the ground. The fairy held up the large, bloody chunk of flesh he had torn from the killer's back and shoulder. Then, in her dream, Amelia realized, for the first time, that the knife came down from inside the Circle.

The killer was someone who had moved past The Coven's Circle of Protection and into the center of the Circle undetected; something only a Witch could do.

The men of The Organization continued their ceremony, and absorbed what Amelia was dreaming, as it became clearer in their minds' eye. They watched as, once again, she saw the look in the fairy's eyes as he raised the chunk of flesh torn from the culprit. Then she flashed on the image of Grace's body falling to the earth over and over and over again, while Summer screamed and Amelia stood motionless.

As if reacting to Amelia's dream, Summer sat straight up in bed in a panic.

PART THREE

chapter 37

October 31, Samhain, Night of the Full Blood Moon

The sun broke over fresh falling snow, just beginning to blanket the earth. The water on the London streets had turned to ice and all was quiet as the day began. October 31, the twenty-eighth birthday of Amelia Pivens Kreutzer, the Pagan New Year known as Samhain and the Full Blood Moon had come. At 11:02 p.m. that evening, the moon would arrive at its closest point to the earth and the world would know if this girl was, in fact, "The One."

If she was the girl in the legend then, at 11:02 p.m. Amelia would be infused with "The Ultimate Power"—a power strong enough to wipe out the opposing Witch in her bloodline and end the Civil War of the Witches; strong enough to bring an end to The Organization, their six-hundred-year killing spree, and the rogue group within them; and strong enough to shift the universal balance of good and evil for the betterment of the universe, and therefore The Craft, forever.

It was not only the coming of "The One" that made the day special. It was a day of celebration for the Witches, the Celts, the Druids, and all Pagans. Samhain is a celebration of both life and death, when all the spirits waiting to be reborn are invited back to earth to celebrate the New Year with their living relatives. It is the end of the last season on the eight-tiered Pagan sabbat wheel and the beginning of the first; an important day for both Witches and Wiccans on many levels, in many ways.

With all of the many things the day represented, there was much to do and Summer had started early. She'd awakened at midnight, reacting to the energy from Amelia's dream, and decided that the day had arrived so she would get up and dive into the work ahead of her. She didn't mind the early start. She enjoyed it actually. She liked being one of few awake, while so many rested.

A ringing alarm woke Amelia at seven. She sat straight up in bed, jumped up and ran into Summer's room. It was empty. The smell of burning sage coming from downstairs hit her.

She's cleansing the house. Amelia ran down the stairs and into the kitchen, where Summer was preparing for the night ahead of them.

"Who ever killed my mother was strong enough to walk into the Circle of Protection, undetected. It wasn't The Organization. It was another Witch—someone who knew her ways, her weak points."

Summer looked up from the cauldron on the stove, where she was busy adding rosemary. "Good morning," she said, calmly.

"It was another Witch. I know it and so does Jeremy."

"What are you saying?"

"That it was another Witch."

"No one from The Coven killed your mother. Please, don't even think that."

"I don't. Not exactly."

"Not exactly?"

"There is someone pretending to be with us. Someone studied Mom enough to walk into that Circle and attack her."

"Whoever killed your mother risked his life to jump into the Circle with his knife raised. I'm sure he died before the night was over."

"How do you know?"

"Because it was a strong Circle. I was there. So were you."

"Right, and neither of us know what really happened. I saw it in my dream last night, Summer. I saw the blade come at her from inside the Circle."

"You were dreaming."

"Yes, I was … *and* I was remembering. I know Summer. I know that Jeremy has a secret he's keeping and I know it has something to do with that night."

"Your problems with Jeremy are a separate issue."

"I don't think so. I didn't tell you everything I saw that night at his house because I didn't quite understand it all, but I do now. There was something around him. A secret. Jeremy was hiding in the shadows of who he is. I couldn't tap into it, but in my vision it came through as black smoke. He didn't reveal the entire secret, but I saw he had one and I didn't understand what it was until my dream last night."

"So, you saw part of a secret?"

"I remembered a moment from my childhood. He was talking to me about The Craft behind my father's back."

"How old were you?"

"Eight or nine."

"Do you remember that incident happening in reality?"

"No."

"So, it could have been your subconscious asking you to consider something or the Goddess giving you a symbol?"

"A symbol of what?"

"I don't know. Was Jeremy hurting you in the vision?"

"No."

"Was he protective or fatherly?"

"Fatherly, I suppose."

"Sometimes fathers lie to their children to protect them."

"But he was going behind my father's back. He lied to him."

"Because he knew this day would come. He knew that if he taught you the ways of The Craft indirectly, eventually they would help you. And if that is what he did, then it worked. You have reentered, as though you never left."

"Outside of my ability to separate my emotions."

"Yes. There was nothing that could be done about that. Jeremy has kept things from you, but he hasn't betrayed you and he would never do anything to hurt your mother. I don't see any connection between him and the night your mother was killed. I think your emotions and your frustrations about what you don't know are clouding the issue again."

"I'm not saying he did it, but I think he knows who did." Amelia wouldn't let up. She didn't understand her feelings, but she knew that Jeremy's lies ran deep and he was not to be trusted. She could feel it in her bones. "It was another Witch who killed her. I'm sure of it. When I saw Jeremy, in the vision, there was a darkness seeping out of him. There was a thick, black smoke coming out of his mouth as though his soul was black and all his words were lies. That black smoke signified a dark secret having to do with me and everything that he's lied about. That vision was about him hiding something."

"The dark secret you saw Jeremy hiding could have been what he told you last night."

"That my mother confronted The Organization? So did I. What I saw was bigger than that. You don't understand."

"Yes, I do. And the secret you saw in Jeremy, you should have seen in me, too. Maybe you didn't because we've only just met and it's not something I was necessarily hiding because I have never once felt compelled to tell you ..."

Amelia leaned back against a counter, arms crossed, her manner demanding an explanation. "What?"

Summer let her shoulders fall. She closed her eyes and ran her hands through her hair. "Okay," Summer said, giving up the fight. "You know, sometimes we keep things from each other out of love, but I can see you're not going to let me do that."

"No. I'm not."

"It's not just that your mother went to The Organization, Amelia. She went there to make a deal," Summer looked into her eyes, not wanting to hurt Amelia, but having no choice. "Your mother went to The Organization and traded her life for yours. Someone got into The Circle that night because she let them in. I'm sorry."

Amelia was speechless. She didn't say a word. She simply sat down, not taking her eyes off of Summer.

"She believed that if she gave them what she thought they wanted from her, then they would leave you alone. She offered her life and she offered the rogue group insight into her magickal abilities. She taught them."

"No, she didn't."

"Yes, Amelia, she did, but it wasn't much—nothing they could really hurt anyone with. You must understand that, as a mother, she felt this was something she had to do."

"No."

"She knew they were watching you—we all did—but we thought it was just for your extraordinary magickal abilities. We didn't think they would find out who you really were. Back then, no one realized just how much information The Organization had about the legend of 'The One'—that it might be a real possibility—but, as it turns out, they knew everything. If she had known that, she wouldn't have made any deals. She would have known that leaving you was exactly what they wanted.

"There are many painful things that Jeremy never told you, and for good reason. It's all in the past and there has never been any point in bringing any more sorrow into your life. Now you know what happened. He's family to you, Amelia. Jeremy loves you."

Amelia was stunned. Tears rolled down her face at the thought of the sacrifice her mother made for her, but there was still something about the story that felt incomplete. She knew there was more—something else she didn't know.

"I know Jeremy loves me, Summer ... but, as he's said, and as you've said, there is me, Amelia, the woman—and then there is me, the symbol of an extraordinary turning point that will change the future of Witchcraft forever. Who I am to The Craft is more important to him than who I am as a person ... No matter how much he loves me, I come second."

"That isn't a fair way to look at it," Summer said, becoming frustrated with Amelia.

"That doesn't mean it isn't the right way," Amelia said. "You taught me that. I have to think of the greater good of the universe before myself, right?"

"Look," Summer said with both frustration and compassion, "you can't do this. I know there's a lot to explain, that you need to know your history and that you want all the answers, but you've got to give it some time. I can't just sit down and fill you in on the entire history of The Craft, Wicca and your family, over afternoon tea."

"Try me."

"No. That approach will only confuse you and, at the end of the day, you won't really know anything. You have to be patient, Amelia. You have to accept the fact that you don't know everything and, until you do, you've got to trust us."

"If his lies were well-intentioned, then why the black smoke?"

"That is a question only Isis and your memories can answer. But remember, visions are often symbols—not literal translations of a particular situation."

Amelia didn't reply but was, clearly, still unsatisfied.

"We've reached the day and it's come fast," Summer said, getting down to business. "Do you think you can put aside your doubts so that tonight we can guide you through the experience of taking in this great power?"

"Do I have a choice?" Amelia asked.

"Not really. You know, maybe Jeremy has lied to you and maybe I have too, but the only people you should be fighting right now are the ones who are out to destroy you and the ones who will try to control you once you take in the power of 'The One.'"

"I understand."

"Good."

"So … What will it be like?"

"What?"

"Taking in 'The Ultimate Power'? Becoming 'The One'?"

"I have no idea."

* * *

Amelia looked around the kitchen. She swallowed her feelings and calmed down enough to realize that all the counters and the breakfast table were covered with supplies for their evening. She walked through the kitchen looking at everything. She'd always loved the preparation as a child. Getting ready for the big celebrations was something she'd looked forward to for months in advance.

A large candle sat in a cauldron. It would be burned that night to represent the Samhain fire. It was a fire to clear away the brush and it represented the changing seasons. In regions where a bonfire was not appropriate, a candle was placed in a cauldron as a symbol of the clearing. On the table next to it there were three bowls—one of fresh ginger, one of cinnamon and one of basil—all traditional spices and herbs used on Samhain. Three glass vials of oil sat among a number of carved pumpkins, aster flowers, bright red apples, homemade orange candles and a black cloth that would be used to cover their altar that night. Amelia picked up one of the vials, opened it, and held it under her nose. It was cinnamon, galangal root, peppermint, dried rue, vervain, essential oil and sunflower oil. She remembered the scent, but she didn't know why. "What is this for?"

"Protection."

"There are three vials."

"One for each of us," Summer smiled.

Amelia started to dab hers on.

"Not yet," Summer said, stopping her.

"I need to take a protection bath first, don't I?"

Summer nodded.

"It's all coming back to me."

"I cleaned the house with War Water this morning and made a bath of it for you."

"War Water. What am I supposed to do?" Amelia said, with hesitation.

"Fully immerse yourself, three times, and then towel off."

"Did you already do it?"

"Yes, I did."

"The water is cold, isn't it?"

"Yes. Sorry about that," Summer went to the stove, removed a kettle of boiling water, and made Amelia a cup of tea. "Warm yourself from the inside before you dunk."

"Thank you," she said and took the cup. "This is boldo."

"Yes."

"Where did you get it?"

"Our network contact in Chile sends it to me."

"This was my mother's favorite. She drank it every day. She even brought it in a thermos when we went to the park."

"She did?"

Amelia nodded. "She said it was good for your skin."

"Yes, but in Witchcraft, its primary use is warding off stalkers," Summer said, surprised that she never knew this about Grace.

Amelia's eyes widened and her mind raced. This was something she'd never heard before.

"She drank it every day?" Summer asked again.

Amelia nodded, remembering the afternoon of the day her mother was killed. She'd had a feeling that they weren't alone in the park, but dismissed it because Grace seemed to have no sense of the presence. "That's why you had boldo leaves all around the house the other night?"

"Yes, but it's also got a great flavor and your mother was known to indulge herself with certain luxuries. This was probably one of them."

"Probably," Amelia said, uncomfortably, as she looked to all the activity on the stove. "What else is going on over here?" She took a lid off a pot. "Mmm. Elderberry wine."

"It's all good stuff."

"Yes. This is the fun part." She took the lid off of another small cauldron, but couldn't figure out what it was. "Don't tell me. Let's see, we've got some basil, rosemary, Saint John's Wort ... I don't know this one. What are you making?" Amelia asked as her eyes fell on a small jar next to the stove.

She opened it and examined the contents. "Wolfsbane," Amelia said. "This is pretty toxic. What are you doing with it?" she asked with a hint of suspicion.

"A Calendar Oracle," Summer answered, knowing better than to try and hide it from Amelia.

"You're going to ask a question."

Summer nodded.

"And what is the question?"

"I haven't decided, yet. That's why the Wolfsbane is still in the jar."

"Oh."

"But if I do ... if I ask *that* question, do you want to know the answer?"

"No. And Summer. I don't want you to ask that question. Those readings aren't always right and I don't want any confusion. As the moon draws closer, the true answer of who I am will be revealed, okay?"

"Okay."

Amelia opened the oven. "Ooh. Is this what I think it is?"

"Pumpkin cake."

"What's that for?"

"Your birthday."

Amelia turned to find Summer holding a gift.

"But, I don't celebrate my birthday, Summer."

"Then celebrate Samhain."

Amelia recognized the gift wrap. "It's Chanel."

"But, of course. So, are you going to tell me that you don't want it?"

Amelia smiled. She took the box, quickly untied the ribbons and opened the package. It was a black silk and velvet wrap with black beading.

"It's for tonight. It matches your dress."

"It does and I love it. Thank you! How do you know what my dress looks like?"

"I knew you were a Chanel girl, so I figured if I went down there, someone would know you."

"You met Diana."

"I did."

"It's just beautiful, Summer. Thank you."

"You're welcome."

Amelia scanned the kitchen. "So what can I help with?"

"All that's left is making the sabbat wheel, but that's my favorite part, so I'm all set."

"Okay."

"And you, my dear, have many other things to do."

"The War Water."

"Yes, but there's one more thing first," Summer got an apple and a knife and handed it to Amelia.

"It's not time yet."

"Sure it is."

Amelia sliced the apple in half and looked at it. The seeds of an apple cut crosswise are arranged in a five pointed star, a pentagram.

Summer leaned over to see. "Two seeds showing. Two tasks and two, only, for you."

"Two is enough. And, I suppose, the first is the War Water."

"It will be quick. Cold and quick. Three full body dunks. It's good for you."

"Easy for you to say."

"I did it, too."

"I know."

Amelia started up to the bathroom, then turned and went back to the kitchen, unable to dismiss her mother's visit to The Organization. "Did my father know what she did?"

"No. We promised her he never would."

"So he didn't know that she was in England?"

"He thought she was on a retreat in Lake Tahoe. Everyone did. Jeremy didn't even know she was here until after she left."

"What about my dream? About the murderer coming from within the Circle? Even if it has nothing to do with Jeremy, I dreamt it."

"She made a deal with The Organization, so she expected them. She obviously left a weak spot in the Circle for them so they could get in. That would explain your dream. And the fact that Jeremy and I knew about the deal explains your black smoke.

"It couldn't have been another Witch? A descendent from the other side?"

"I don't think so. I'll talk to Jeremy about it, but regardless of what happened, your mother's murder is an issue of the past. You've got to move on Amelia, just like with Wolfgang."

"I will."

"You must."

Summer held up the apple. "And I think your two tasks are The National Gallery, and embracing this special night—not Jeremy, not me—not anything of the past."

"Got it."

"Good. Now, you need the War Water, then the oil," Summer handed her the vial. "Carry it with you today. The forces working against you have already begun their preparations."

Amelia looked into Summer's eyes "I'm ready."

"I know you are."

chapter 38

The National Gallery, London
Trafalgar Square Entrance, 9 a.m.

A security guard placed a sign that read, "The National Gallery, London, Closed Today For Private Event" at the bottom of the stairs leading up to the Gallery from Trafalgar Square. He looked across the plaza, breathing in the cold air and watching as the first snow of the year began to fall, then he went inside to get warm.

The National Gallery, London
Loading Dock, Same Time

Jeremy walked outside, into the snow, wrapped in a black coat and scarf. He looked around. He was waiting for someone.

Claude approached the Gallery while he sipped his morning coffee. As he neared the loading dock entrance, he saw Jeremy and stopped, watching him from a distance as another man in a tailored coat approached him. It was Francis Brunning, the head of The Organization.

Jeremy and Francis said nothing. They simply shook hands, neither of them taking their eyes off of the other. Then Jeremy reached under his coat, took out a stack of invitations for the

Goya opening, and handed them to Francis. Jeremy went inside, Francis disappeared down a nearby alley, and Claude finished his coffee and walked toward the building.

The National Gallery, East Wing
Goya Exhibit, 10 a.m.

Amelia arrived at the Gallery full of energy. She had nothing but positive thoughts about what the evening would bring, primarily because that's what she'd managed to talk herself into.

She would allow her beloved Goya and her born gift of The Craft to guide her through the inevitable, which was only hours away. She joined Martel and Jeremy, who were supervising as *The Naked Maja* was being hung next to *The Clothed Maja*.

"Thank God," Amelia said to Martel. "There's nothing like last-minute arrivals."

"I was beginning to worry."

"So was I. Good morning."

"Happy Birthday," Jeremy said giving her a hug. "I thought you'd be here at the crack of dawn."

"So did I, but I was in a very deep sleep last night." She studied the side-by-side *Majas*. "One woman. Two conflicting truths."

"Or two women for the price of one," Jeremy said. "No gentleman would think twice."

Amelia smiled wryly. "Yes, but with women like that you've really got to watch your back, don't you?"

Jeremy looked to Amelia, letting her know that he understood the subtext of her words and she knew it was time to redirect the conversation. "Are the cabinet paintings up?" she asked.

"Yes," Claude's voice called out as he hurried over to them. "Mr. Roth, you have a call waiting."

"Thank you, Claude. I'll see you all tonight," Martel nodded and looked to his watch as Jeremy disappeared down the hall.

"Mrs. Kreutzer."

"Señor Demingo."

"Everything looks wonderful. Thank you."

"No. Thank you. This exhibit wouldn't be what it is, were it not for *The Prado.*"

"A good decision all the way around … Well, I have an appointment. I should get going."

"Have a good day Señor Demingo."

"Thank you. You, too."

Martel left and Amelia turned to Claude, "Show me the way."

"Of course, Madam."

She followed Claude through the East Wing. "I can't believe how quickly we've made this happen," she said.

"I'm just happy everything is here."

"Me too."

They walked into a side room in the East Wing to find Goya's *The Shipwreck, The Fire At Night* and *Interior of a Prison.* Amelia took them in. "They're all intended to represent danger approaching chaos."

"Well, he met with success there didn't he?"

"Yes."

"It's interesting that he did three paintings and they always say bad things happen in threes. Do you think he knew that?"

"That's a good question. I'm not sure, but it makes sense."

"Well, there's much to do so I better be moving along here."

"Yes. It's a busy day. I'll see you later … and Claude," she wrapped her hand around his, "Thank you for all your help and support. I couldn't have done it without you, and you really are a good friend."

"As are you, Madam."

* * *

Goya, Goya, Goya! While going over her fantasy of the perfect evening in her head, Amelia walked through the administrative halls toward her office. *This is going to be good. An artistic extravaganza! And it's going to be fun and I'm going to deal with that other matter starting at 10:45 p.m. and not one minute sooner.*

With a beaming smile of confidence, she turned the corner to find Jeremy sneaking out of her office with a large shopping bag from the museum store. Her body tensed. "Jeremy!" He continued walking as though he didn't hear her, although she knew it was impossible that he didn't.

"Jeremy, stop!"

Amelia was panicked. She started to run after him when someone approached her from behind and took her arm. She screamed and whipped around to find Martel.

"Are you okay, Señora?"

"Yes. Yes, I'm fine," she said quickly, wanting to go after Jeremy. "You just startled me is all, but I ..."

Martel cut her off. "I'm sorry ... and I'm sorry that my words were so harsh the other night."

"It's okay. You have priceless art here and I'm clearly having some personal problems. I'm sorry too ... I'd thought you'd gone."

"Yes, I'm leaving. I just ... I ..."

"Yes? Is something wrong?"

"I don't have a partner for the evening and I wondered if?"

"Of course. Yes. But we'll have to meet here. Is that alright?"

"Yes. Thank you. And Happy Birthday."

"Thank you, Señor Demingo. I really do have to get to my office."

"Tonight, then."

"Tonight."

Martel turned to walk away and Amelia ran down the hall and into her office. She locked the door behind her and went directly to the trunk of Isis. She opened it to find it was empty. She was immediately consumed by fear and suspicion about what Jeremy might be doing and why. What if he did have something to do with her mother's death? What if he was going to do something to hurt her? She hated the thought, but it's what she kept coming back to and she knew there was a reason for that. Something about Jeremy just wasn't right.

Amelia was scared. For a moment she couldn't move and seemed to stop breathing. Then she snapped and all her emotions poured out at once. She was suddenly hysterical. She picked up the phone and started to dial, then hung it up. "No. No phones.

Oh, my God." She started to walk toward the door and threw up all over the floor in one violent and uncontrolled spasm. She began to cry. "What is he doing?"

Amelia stopped. She stopped herself from panicking as her paranoia set in. She checked the door to make sure it was locked, then carefully looked around the room, as if to make sure no one was watching. She didn't see anything unusual, but she still didn't feel secure. She drew a Circle of Protection around herself with her finger and closed her eyes, envisioning a pentagram on her forehead for further protection. Once she was in the safety of the Circle, Amelia let herself crumble to the floor. She was too full of confusion and fear to do anything else. She took the oil that Summer prepared from her pocket, rubbed it in her hands, then up through her hair and scalp as she rocked back and forth crying.

"Why? Why? Why is this real?" she pleaded, completely unaware that a lipstick camera had been placed in an air vent. From the comfort of an office at The Organization, Francis and Dorian were sitting behind a monitor, sipping their tea and watching her—not that knowing would have mattered to Amelia, at that point. She was finally, truly breaking down emotionally. She remained in the Circle, in the same position, for almost four hours, letting her mind go and her body collapse; wondering what it was she was supposed to do next and damning whichever God or Goddess or Devil or All gave her this life.

With each passing moment Dorian became more excited at what an easy puppet Amelia would be to handle, but Francis was concerned. He was afraid this was an indication that she might not be strong enough to accept the gift the universe was to bestow on her when the Full Blood Moon arrived and that was something he just couldn't afford. Amelia had to pull herself together for all of them.

She finally looked up at the clock to see it was almost four. In a split-second she gathered her thoughts. She was sharp again. She jumped up and ran from her office at lightening speed. "Good girl," Francis said as she disappeared from the monitor. "You keep on fighting luv. You just keep on fighting."

chapter 39

Summer was dressed and ready for the Goya opening. Her long blonde hair flowed over her deep green dress and fell just beyond her waist. With her delicate features and romantic accessories, she was a beauty right out of the Renaissance. Summer was energized. She was fueled by the excitement of what could happen that night and who they would all be by sunset on November the first.

She was packing up everything she'd made for the celebration and ceremony when Amelia burst through the door in a panic—with no coat on, smelling like vomit and the oil that soaked her hair. "Jeremy stole everything. I saw him."

Summer dropped the bowl she was holding.

"All of my mother's things. They've been hidden in my office for years and no one ever knew. No one even knew that I had them. No one at all—not even my father."

"Honey," Summer said, carefully taking Amelia's hands in hers—afraid she might react to her touch. "I need you to calm down, Amelia. You've got to breathe."

"It took ..." Amelia started to cry and her breathing was so erratic that she couldn't get the words out.

Summer guided her to a chair and pushed her head down between her knees. "Breathe." She poured Amelia a glass of water.

Amelia sipped the water and was finally calm enough to start again. "It took another Witch to get into that Circle and kill my mother. She didn't make a deal to be murdered right in front of me. I don't believe that. There's more. I don't know if he did it, but I know Jeremy isn't being truthful with us. This is beyond protecting me. He wants something."

"Just hold on. Let's figure out exactly what's going on, before we decide that his motivations, for whatever he's doing, are bad."

"What is wrong with you?! Don't you see what's happening here? Can't you feel it?!"

"I think Jeremy is going about things the wrong way, but that's the way he's been doing it your whole life. I also think you're very sensitive to events because you're feeling a lot of energy that is both positive and negative. This is an overwhelming day, but you've got to realize that not even a fraction of that energy is coming from Jeremy. You have a body and a mind that changes and intensifies with the moon. You are a woman, much more complicated than most, and you've got a lot to learn before you can overcome these intense feelings and sensations. Jeremy has grown accustomed to not telling you what's going on and, as he's said—and as I've said—many feel that the fate of all Witches lies in what this night delivers—or doesn't deliver. This isn't about one man out to get another. You must understand that, for the protection of all Witches, and for your own peace of mind. He could very well be doing something to help. If I'd known you had all of your mother's tools I'd want to use them, too."

"Why aren't you hearing me?!"

"I am hearing you, Amelia, and I will handle Jeremy, but you have got to get it together. I can't say it any more. If you don't calm down by 11:02 p.m., then The Organization and the opposing Witches will have stepped in and we'll all be dead by sunset tomorrow. Our only unpredictable obstacle is your emotional state and we can't have that. Do you understand me?!"

"Yes."

"Good." Summer picked up a garment bag off the counter. "Chanel had it delivered when you didn't show up. Diana said to call her if you need a different size."

Amelia took the bag.

"I will go and see Jeremy and we'll meet you at the party."

"You can't go to his house alone."

"Of course I can," she said with force, "and believe me, Amelia, with all that's going on tonight, the sooner you realize Jeremy is not the root of your problems, the better."

Amelia just stood there, looking at her. "Get in the shower … right now." Amelia lingered for a moment and then ran up the stairs to follow Summer's orders.

chapter 40

Residence of Jeremy Roth, 6 p.m.

Summer cut the headlights on her car, as she slowly rolled up to Jeremy's house and parked under the camouflage of a cluster of trees. She wanted to see what he was doing before she announced herself. She knew that Amelia was overwhelmed by her growing sixth sense, and that she didn't have it under control, but she didn't want to doubt the girl's instinct. If there was a problem with Jeremy, Summer would have to find a way to deal with it, and it would be much easier if he didn't know she was aware of it.

She quietly walked toward a window of the room where she, Amelia and Jeremy had performed the ritual of Amelia's renewed faith. She stepped up on a rock and peered in. Her eyes widened and her body tensed. There was a ceremony taking place and Señor Martel Demingo was performing it. He was alone, surrounded by magickal candles, standing before a mummified body and photographs of Summer and Amelia.

Summer was stunned. She watched, unsure of exactly what he was doing. He picked up a length of rope and began a spell, by tying it in knots, as he recited.

> *With this first knot,*
> *this spell I tie.*

This magick will hold.
It will not die.
This second knot,
will make it true.
You divide from her
and she from you.
Through this knot of three,
you will see.
The magick will breathe
as blessed by thee …

Summer's heart pounded. Martel was performing a spell to divide Summer and Amelia, to turn them against each other.

Summer scanned the room and property outside. There was no sign of Jeremy. She didn't know if that was good or bad. She quietly hurried back to her car. Short of breath, with shaking hands, she barely managed to turn the key. She drove away, too distraught to realize that a car from The Organization had pulled out behind her from the shadows in Jeremy's driveway. She was too distraught to realize that Martel was in the window watching both her and the black town car drive away.

chapter 41

The National Gallery, London, 7 p.m.

Amelia was a picture of elegance in a black Chanel gown that blended with her hair and showcased her green eyes. She entered the Gallery through the public doors and walked quickly through the museum. She hurried past *The Spell, The Dream/Sleep of Reason* and *The Duchess of Alba*, whose eyes seemed to follow her as she turned down the hall toward The National Gallery's administrative offices. Her pace didn't let up until she reached Jeremy's closed door, where she stopped. She stood for a moment to contemplate, and to catch her breath. She knew that Summer was with him and she was sure she'd have at least a half-hour to search Jeremy's office—for what, exactly, she didn't know.

Amelia looked around to be sure no one was watching and then slowly opened the door. The smell of incense poured into the hall. The office was not empty. Jeremy was cloaked in copper velvet and performing a ritual with her mother's magickal tools. Amelia stood, frozen in place. Jeremy's reaction to Amelia was not sudden. It was as though he expected her—he slowly tilted his head up, leveling his eyes with hers.

It scared her. He knew that. But, the fact of the matter was that he had not foreseen the intrusion and this was a ceremony that he would not be able to explain.

Amelia looked down at a bowl filled with candles, herbs, various oils and photographs of her and Summer. She didn't say anything. She couldn't. Tears of anger and resentment rolled down her face and her hands began to shake with rage as she took in what Jeremy had done. She looked at him—back, deep into his eyes. He'd betrayed her once again.

Jeremy watched, without making a move, as Amelia slowly began to walk around the room, blowing out candles and breaking the tips off the burning incense sticks. She didn't take her eyes off him. She wouldn't. She knew, now, that her instincts had been right about Jeremy having a dark secret. Now she was searching for the reason, for his intention and most of all, for his secret.

chapter 42

Residence of Amelia Pivens Kreutzer, 7:15 p.m.

Summer arrived back at the flat, parked on the sidewalk and flew through the door screaming, "Amelia!" She ran through the house looking for her. "Amelia!"

Relieved to find she was already gone, Summer rushed to create a Circle of Protection. She lit two candles, pulled the lace from a nearby shoe and used it to tie the same knots Martel had tied for his spell. Then she began a spell to reverse Martel's, by untying the knots as she recited.

> *Listen to this spell I weave.*
> *To break your wishes,*
> *destroy your deeds.*
> *By the rise of this night's Full Blood Moon.*
> *I will reverse what you have sewn ...*

The sounds of breaking glass came from the kitchen.

Two men from The Organization climbed through the kitchen door and arrived in the front room to find the candles lit and Summer gone. They heard a car screech down the road and ran to the front window, only to see that Summer was all the way down the street. They scanned the house.

One of them found the lace on the floor. He picked it up and smiled. There were two knots in it. Martel had tied nine. She hadn't reversed the spell. She hadn't even had the time to delay its effects.

chapter 43

Jeremy Roth's Office, 7:30 p.m.

Jeremy and Amelia were on opposite sides of the room, stepping sideways as they moved, as though they were hunting each other in some bizarre and ritualistic manner.

"You don't know everything, Amelia, and that is for your own protection."

"That's not good enough."

"Maybe not, but you're missing twenty years of practice. This is going to take time."

"Why is that? If I am this 'One,' then, why?"

"Just because you have the power, doesn't mean you'll know how to use it or who the players are."

"I'm beginning to get a pretty good idea of who's who."

"You don't understand the circumstances you're in, yet. No one expects you to. You weren't raised to be who you are."

"Who you *think* I am ... and, if I am her, what is it that you get?"

"I'm sorry?"

"Surely there's a personal gain for you."

Jeremy moved closer to her. "That is not the foundation of The Craft, Amelia. There is much about your mother and this world that you have to learn."

"But, I'm a natural. Isn't that right? What can someone with my inherent power learn from you?"

"Quite a bit. If you survive to receive that power."

"Is that a threat?"

"More a simple reality, I would say."

"Would you?" Amelia slowly walked across the room toward Jeremy. "I know that it took another Witch to get into that Circle and kill my mother. In a state that intuitive, there is no way a man of The Organization would have gone unnoticed, even if she left a window for them. Someone would have felt it. I would have."

"Amelia."

"How exactly did you meet her?"

"It was by correspondence, only. And there are a great many things about your mother's practice that I must explain. I realize you've caught me in a rather compromising and confusing setting, but I promise you that things are not exactly as they seem to be." As Jeremy moved his hands to take down the hood of his cloak, Amelia noticed that he was wearing a copper ring. She was taken back, as this was another signature of her mother's. Jeremy saw her reaction. "My use of copper is a symbol of your mother— to pay tribute," he said.

"It's a symbol of my mother's power, Jeremy. Is that what this is about? Is that what you're after? Power?" She looked back to the photos of Amelia and Summer that were in the Circle and then she took note of the various tools he was using. She slowly backed up, toward the door, not taking her eyes off Jeremy. "This is a separation spell that you're doing, isn't it? To separate me from Summer. To turn us against each other."

"Yes."

"You want her out of the way," she said, trying to show no fear in being alone.

"Yes."

"And my mother? Did you want her out of the way too?"

"Amelia."

"Did you?!"

"Hasn't Summer told you that your mother went to The Organization? Traded her life for yours?"

"We both know that isn't true."

"Isn't it? Do you think Summer would lie to you?"

Amelia didn't answer him.

"Why would she do that, Amelia? Why on earth would Summer lie to you about something like that?" he said, suggesting that that's exactly what she'd done.

"I'm not going to address that implication."

"Not a wise choice, my dear."

"You always have to be the one in control, don't you?"

"I'm just trying to get you to let go of the past and see the future, the present. You must do that now. You must let all of this go."

Amelia turned to leave and Jeremy grabbed her arm with force, spinning her around and cornering her against a wall. "You will not walk out on me."

"It was you. You killed her to get to me. You're the one who wants my magick. You're worse than The Organization. You're worse than all of them."

"I've waited patiently, Amelia. I've carefully planned your life and dedicated mine to yours. This night has been hundreds of years in the making … It's not time for you to fight with me, but to listen and learn. You will not jeopardize …"

Amelia's eyes shifted and, in one swift move, she grabbed her mother's athame and plunged it into Jeremy's shoulder, missing his heart by little more than an inch. He fell to the floor. He was still breathing, but losing a great deal of blood. Amelia stared at him, mildly shocked, but feeling completely justified by what she'd just done. Tears of disbelief ran down her face at his betrayal.

"I did listen and learn, Jeremy … and you taught me so much that—here we are."

Claude was doing a final walk-through of the exhibit when Amelia stabbed Jeremy. He'd stopped, abruptly, the moment Jeremy's knees buckled and his body collapsed to the floor. It was as though he'd sensed what happened. Then, Claude turned to the painting beside him. It was *All Will Fall*, a portrayal of the mighty bogeyman, shrunken into a manipulated marionette—an artistic reminder that someone else is always in control, and nothing is ever what it seems to be.

chapter 44

7:55 p.m.

Martel, sharply dressed in a tuxedo, left Jeremy's house in a black limousine, as a string of black town cars and limousines left The Organization.

Summer sat in her car, which she'd stopped on Trafalgar Square. She was still trying to catch her breath. She didn't want to arrive at Amelia's event showing any fear. That's not what Amelia needed, and it certainly wouldn't help anything. She looked up at The National Gallery and then took notice of the Full Blood Moon. It was bright orange, a breathtaking sight, shining over London and creating an eerie reflection on the snow.

Summer reminded herself to breathe as she looked deeper into the moon, looking for the Goddess, looking for help. "If there is any God or Goddess to support me, any entity that can aide in whatever this night becomes, I implore you … the time to redirect the future of The Craft is now and all of the good power of the universe is necessary." She closed her eyes and prayed.

She tried not to cry. For the first time since she'd arrived in London, Summer had doubts. She looked and felt as if she might be defeated.

chapter 45

The National Gallery, London, East Wing, 8:00 p.m.

Claude and Amelia stood by the door together, looking into the painting that would greet the guests as they walked in. *Truth, Time and History* was an angelic oil on canvas that, in no way, prepared viewers for the works that would surround them as they moved deeper and deeper into the exhibit, eventually concluding with the dramatic presentation of *Quinta del Sordo*.

Claude took Amelia's hand, hoping to calm her nerves. "You're fooling them with this one. It's so beautiful, but once they get past that ..."

"They're neck-deep in the human condition."

"Where is Mr. Roth?"

"I don't know," Amelia said calmly ... so much so, that she surprised herself. "He might be with Martel."

"I expected both of them to be right here when the doors opened."

"So did I."

"Maybe they're letting you go solo. It is your night, and you do deserve to be queen."

"Thank you."

"Shall we?" He motioned toward the door.

Amelia nodded and two guards opened the doors to the exhibit.

Amelia let the crowd pass by her, greeting many of the people she knew, as they arrived. Then she strolled through the Gallery on her own, watching London's elite wander around in awe of the artist and his works before them.

Martel approached her with a glass of champagne. "You look stunning."

"Thank you."

He raised his glass. "To Goya."

"To Goya."

They drank to their treasured artist only to be interrupted by Detective Carlisle.

"Good evening, Detective. Is everything alright?" Amelia asked.

"I'm sorry to interrupt. May I have a moment?"

"Of course."

"Excuse me," Martel said, catching an unfriendly glare from the detective.

"Yes. I'm sorry," Amelia said. "Don't go far."

"I won't," he said as he watched Amelia and the detective step away from the crowd.

"We found your father."

"Oh, thank God."

"Less than an hour ago. Whoever took his body put it back right where they found it."

"In the funeral home?"

He looked into her eyes, again searching for the truth of how much she really knew. "And that's not all."

Amelia took a deep breath. "What is it?"

"Your father's body has been mummified."

"I beg your pardon?" she said, in a tone convincing the detective that she was truly shocked.

"It was a traditional mummification—like they did on the Pharaohs of Egypt, to ensure they had a safe journey into the afterlife. For Egyptians, it's very respectful—an honor."

"Yes. I know."

"Someone was trying to ensure a safe journey for your father."

Amelia's mind was racing. *Who would do this? Why?*

"So, he's back at the funeral home now?" she asked.

"Yes."

Not knowing what else to do, Amelia shook his hand. "Thank you very much, Detective. You can stay for the party if you like."

"I need you to come to Scotland Yard, first thing in the morning."

"Yes. First thing."

"Are you alright, Mrs. Kreutzer?"

"I'll be fine. It's just a lot to deal with … You've just told me that my father's body was mummified, it's the biggest night of my career, and it's my birthday for, God's sake. I don't know if it's possible to be alright."

"I'm referring to your safety, Mrs. Kreutzer. I'm concerned that there is quite a bit going on here that I am not yet aware of."

"It's just my big night, Detective."

"Yes it is, isn't it? The exhibit, Samhain, the Full Blood Moon."

Amelia was surprised by his words, but did her best to show him no reaction.

He read her reservation immediately. "There is quite a bit I'm not aware of, Madam, but there is also quite a bit of which *I am* aware."

They held each other's gaze for a long moment. Amelia was still trying to play it cool, but realized that she was not doing a terribly good job.

"Once again, Mrs. Kreutzer, I am referring to your safety. Is there a reason that I should stay at this party?"

"No, Detective, but thank you."

"I'm on your side, Amelia."

"I know and I appreciate that very much. Have a good evening."

He looked the room over, as though everyone in it was a suspect in a crime of which he was not yet aware, but soon would be.

"Goodnight Mrs. Kreutzer," he said, finally. He turned and walked out the main entrance with no intention of going very far. Detective Carlisle had come to know when things were close to happening and he knew that whatever was going to transpire that night was big, it was coming quickly, and it involved Amelia.

chapter 46

Summer walked into the Gallery, passing Detective Carlisle
as he left the party. She spotted Amelia and went straight toward
her, careful to keep a cheerful look on her face, for the sake of the
guests. Amelia wrapped her arm around Summer's. "Where have
you been? They found my father's body—mummified."

"I know."

"You know?"

"Well, I thought it was him. When I went to Jeremy's, there
was a mummified body in the center of the ceremony room, and
someone was executing a magickal spell."

"What? Who was?"

"Martel."

"Martel?" Amelia looked over her shoulder at him. "Martel—
from *The Prado*?"

"Yes."

"Are you sure?"

"I didn't want to tell you this before, because I wasn't sure if
he was following you because he was afraid you were jeopardizing
his art, or because he was involved with this."

"He's been following me?"

"Yes."

"Martel?" she repeated, looking to him again. "This man?"

"Yes, him. I hadn't really been following you the day you went to The Organization. I was following Martel. I didn't tell you or Jeremy, because I didn't want to say anything until I knew. And the night that you broke the window in the man's car outside the house …" Amelia's eyes widened. She'd kept that a secret. "I saw it happen, Amelia. It's okay. It didn't surprise me, but Martel was there that night, too. He was parked right across the street, watching you."

"That was the night we saw the men in the car park."

"What men?"

"Martel and I ran into two men from The Organization in the car park. One of them followed me when I left. Martel must have followed us … but I don't know how. I still don't understand."

"He was performing a separation spell at Jeremy's house with your father's body and photographs of you and me. Your father's energy was being used to support the divide. Jeremy wasn't there so I don't know if he realizes."

"He realizes. He was here, doing the same thing."

"What?"

"I came here to search his office and I found him performing a ritual. He was using my mother's magickal tools to separate us, to turn us against each other. It was dark magic."

"He was separating us?" Summer said, becoming visibly nervous. She looked around for Jeremy. "Where is he now? Did he see you?"

"He wanted control over me—the same way The Organization does, Summer."

"Amelia, no."

"I stabbed him with mother's athame."

"No," Summer was beside herself. "Oh, my God. You can't just hurt people, Amelia. Not like that. I don't care who you are. Those who are intended to will fall by their own weight and that of the universe."

Amelia's reaction was nothing but a look. The cold look of a girl who felt trapped, who felt she'd had no choice.

"Where is he now?"

"On the floor of his office."

"Is he alive?" Summer asked, in a panic.

"I don't know."

"Let's go. Come on."

"No," Amelia said stubbornly.

"What?"

"It's done."

"You can't break the rules, Amelia."

"It's over and done. The rules are broken and Jeremy's gone."

"This will come back to you, times three."

"There's a lifetime coming back to me, times three, Summer. Let's just focus on what's ahead of us."

There was no time to second-guess Amelia. The moon was drawing closer by the minute. Summer had to have faith that she was on the right path and follow her. She had to believe that it was the will of the universe that had taken Jeremy out of the equation.

Amelia looked at her watch. "It's ten o'clock."

"We're an hour away."

"So, if I'm not her, then all of this will stop?"

"For the other Witches it will, but not for The Organization, and not for the Law of Three."

"The Organization will kill me if I'm not worth controlling … for the pure sport of it," Amelia said.

"They'll try," Summer admitted.

"But not before the universe tortures me for all of my wrong doings, times three."

"Amelia."

"It's alright, Summer. It's almost a dare at this point."

"A dare?"

"I even wonder what it will take to truly hurt me now."

"Amelia, don't say that. Focus on right now, okay? Do we have roof access for the ceremony?"

"I have the keys."

"Everything is in the car. I'll go out and get it in a few minutes."

Claude noticed the tension in the girls from across the room and walked over. "Opening night jitters?" he asked.

Amelia forced a smile. "No. Not me."

"Everyone is having a good time. There's nothing to worry about here."

"You're right. It's just that Martel was so concerned about security," she said, covering. "He had to know every entrance, exit and alarm code."

"We went over it several times and I assure you, Madam, everything is going to run smoothly as far as my staff is concerned."

"Thank you, Claude."

"It's my job and my pleasure, Madam."

Amelia followed Summer's eyes as she watched Martel take a glass of champagne from a tray and give a nod to Francis Brunning. The man from The Organization had arrived and was now standing across the room.

Amelia's blood ran cold. "Summer."

"I know."

Claude turned to see what they were looking at. "Everything okay?"

Summer put her arm around Amelia. "It's better than okay, Claude. It's perfect, don't you think?"

"I do."

Summer and Amelia casually watched Martel stroll past the exhibit of the *Quinta del Sordo*. Francis followed him. They were on separate paths, but were clearly going outside to meet.

Amelia looked around the room and noticed, now, that there were members of The Organization everywhere, seemingly strategically placed. She was dumbfounded. She'd checked the guest list that morning and security was incredibly tight. *How did they get in without invitations?* As she asked herself this question, a horror arose from the pit of her stomach. *The only people who had access to additional invitations, besides me, were Jeremy and Martel.*

In her weak moment of realization, Amelia felt someone watching her. She turned to find Dorian's eyes fixed on her from across the room. He raised his glass to her and smiled. Amelia was, again,

an animal trapped in a cage—in her own cage this time, and surrounded by people who she had thought could be trusted. She
looked around the room at all the guests, wondering who the
faces of the people she didn't know belonged to—and wondering
just how well she really knew the people that she did recognize.

Summer was focused on Francis and Martel. She wanted to
know where they were going and what they were going to do.
"Could you excuse me for just a moment?"

"Of course," Claude said.

"Where are you going?" Amelia snapped, hardly hiding her
concern.

Summer squeezed Amelia's arm lovingly, wanting, needing her
to calm down. "Outside for a cigarette."

"But … it's so cold," Amelia replied, as calmly as she could manage.

"I'll be right back."

Summer walked toward the coat check, leaving Amelia totally
unnerved.

"I didn't realize she smoked."

"Yes. Well, not that often."

"She's nervous for you. For your big night," Claude said, glancing toward Summer.

"Yes. She is."

"Just like a mother."

"Exactly like a mother."

Claude looked over to a painting hanging across the room
from them. It was part of the *Quinta del Sordo* exhibit. "That's
not something you want hanging in your bedroom," he said, walking toward *Saturn,* a painting of a monstrous God with the lower
half of a man's bloody body protruding from its mouth.

Amelia followed Claude, but also kept her eyes on Summer.
"No," she said. "Can you imagine? This one was on the ground
floor of his house."

"Why did he call it *Saturn?*"

Amelia watched Summer from the corner of her eye. She was
waiting at the coat check. "He didn't, actually. He didn't name it.

The critics did, over the years. They started calling it that because that's who the painting depicts." Amelia's eyes darted from the painting, to Summer, to Claude, and back again, while Claude gazed into the painting.

"Saturn was a Roman God who devoured his children for fear he would be overthrown by them," Amelia said, as her own words provided her with a sudden realization that constricted her chest and grabbed her heart. Suddenly, she felt a pressure in her head and her hearing was distorted. The thought that filled her, put her body into shock.

She turned to Summer and watched as the attendant brought her coat. Amelia was numb with clarity. Jeremy had tried to devour her, as Saturn did his own children, and now there was this woman, this mother-like figure, who she hardly knew. She had dropped her life and traveled thousands of miles to help Amelia—*for what?* The answer was obvious to Amelia and the thought of being right scared her to death. Not only was she in over her head, on this dangerous night but, Amelia knew, at that moment, she was alone.

As the coat attendant leaned in to help Summer, he moved her long hair clear of her collar, exposing the revealing cut of the back of her dress—and the rather large scar on her right shoulder blade that ran down to the middle of her back—the scar that was left by the fairy when he tried to stop Grace's killer.

No one had noticed. No one had noticed, because Summer had been covered in so much of Grace's blood and she'd cried so many tears for her that night, that no one had noticed that she was bleeding, too, and crying from her own pain.

"Wow. He ate his own children because he was afraid they might be more powerful than he was?" Claude continued, while Amelia stood, at a total loss.

"Yes," she answered, not taking her eyes off of Summer. Not even to blink.

Amelia was unable to move and she was unsure of what to do. Then someone took her hand. She turned to find it was Martel. She was scared, then suddenly calm. In another moment of clarity, Amelia saw him. She saw who he really was. Señor Martel Demingo was the same little boy who had stood by her, when no one else would, the night her mother was murdered. He was the child whose heart had ached for her.

Amelia was astonished and totally confused. Without letting go of her hand, Martel reached into his pocket and removed the necklace Amelia had worn that night. It was the tiny replication of her mother's that she had taken it off and thrown at The Coven after her mother was murdered. He placed the necklace in her free hand then raised their clasped hands together.

"I never should have let go."

chapter 47

Amelia was confused, but she felt safe. She held onto Martel's hand as he explained.

"Our mothers were friends. My father moved us back to his family in Spain after that night and we became the network contact in Madrid. Before San Francisco, we'd lived in London for a few years. My mother's family was here. It was your mother who convinced her to move to San Francisco and expand her understanding of The Craft. They met, here in London, when Grace came to talk with The Organization. The day before she went to see them, she stopped at the shop where my mother was giving a reading. They became friends instantly."

Amelia's head was spinning with the overload of information she was getting. "Your mother gave readings at Mysteries?"

"Yes."

"I saw a drawing of a woman there."

"My mother did it the day they met. She says something inspired her during the reading. Your mother was amazing, Amelia. She's helped to make Wicca and Witchcraft tolerated, and in many cases embraced, around the world. Her dream of a world-wide network, providing knowledge and protection, continued to grow after she died. It still does. Jeremy has been a part of that tradition, and so has Claude and many of the guards here at The National Gallery."

Amelia looked to Claude. He removed his hand from his pocket, revealing the copper ring he had on. "We are all with you, Madam."

"Claude?" she said with a shaky voice.

"It's alright," he assured her. "Listen to him. Martel knows everything."

"Please continue," she said, trying to control her emotions.

"We all have the rings in honor of your mother. We wear them when we want to be recognized, just as she did. The spells that Jeremy and I performed tonight, were to give you your mother's strength, your father's love, and to protect you from Summer. She came here to befriend you so that, at 11:02 p.m. tonight, she would be where she needed to be to eliminate you— within the Circle of Protection. She came here to kill you, Amelia— the same way she killed your mother."

Amelia stood, quietly. She feared that everything Martel was saying was true. When she spoke, she was so tense that her words were barely audible. "I don't understand."

"Your mother went to The Organization and made the offer. That much is true—but it was Summer's idea. It's what she wanted. Your mother gone. You without influence."

"But, she came here to kill me?"

"Only if she was sure that you were, in fact, 'The One' and that you would overpower her."

In shock and disbelief, Amelia watched as Summer walked out the doors of the Gallery. Then, one by one, all the members of The Organization filtered out behind her. Amelia looked around the room to see that all the security guards were looking at her and all were showing their copper rings.

As Detective Carlisle began his walk, back to The National Gallery, with a fresh cup of coffee, Summer came down the main steps of the Gallery and into Trafalgar Square. She was following, or rather, unknowingly, being led by Francis Brunning.

Martel stepped in front of Amelia and took both of her hands in his. "The Organization has always watched Summer. When they contacted Jeremy, with photographs proving it was she who

cast the death spell on your father, not them, we decided to form
a plan. The trap was set when Jeremy called her about your father's
passing. Jeremy told her he thought you might turn to her. He
asked her to embrace you—knowing, all the while, that this was
precisely what Summer wanted."

"He knowingly put my life in danger?"

"It was the only way. Otherwise, she would have simply come
here to kill you and, with her power, none of us were sure we
could stop her ... We knew it would only be a matter of time
before you called her. This way, she walked right into our trap—
completely unaware."

"Into what trap, exactly?"

"In an unprecedented union, we have joined with The Organization to rid the world of Summer Karlsen."

"Are you mad? Why would you do such a thing?"

"Because she is the strongest of the opposing Witches."

"What?"

"Your natural enemy. Your greatest threat. She killed your
mother so she could train you and lure you to the other side,
without you ever realizing what she was doing. She hadn't antici-
pated your father moving you back to London ... and, because
she never trained you, and she knew your birthday was coming,
Summer began to worry about the power you might be coming
into. So, not knowing what to do or how to get around Jeremy,
she tried to unite with The Organization to bring you down.

"It was a few years ago—three years, actually. She was there
the night Wolfgang was killed. That car was intended to hit both
of you, so far as Summer knew, although that wasn't the case at
all. The Organization planned to double-cross her. They knew
they could only get to her if her guard was down and, they assumed, in this instance, it would be. She was Dorian's date that
night. They were positioned right next to you and Wolfgang—
close enough for the car to hit Wolfgang and Summer—but leaving you unharmed.

"Then there would be no one opposing you but them. And,
there would be no one on your side but Jeremy, whom they planned

to kill after he taught you the basics of The Craft. But it didn't work out as planned. Summer sensed the danger, the set-up, at the last minute, and broke away from Dorian.

"After that, she threatened to kill you herself, and all of them as well. She was independent and aggressive—she still is—a powerful vigilante for her own cause and a threat to us all. The only living Witch powerful enough to take her out is you—but you're not practiced. That's why The Organization came to us.

"That's why we've come together for this one night—and this night only. All of this, Amelia, was a long time in planning. The Organization is not here to take you—not tonight. Not yet. That was the agreement. In a matter of moments, Summer will be gone and you will be secure in taking in the power meant to be yours. This war with the other side and The Organization is over for now and all is as it should be."

chapter 48

"All is as it should be?" Amelia repeated Martel's words, aloud, to see if what he said would make sense to her, but it still didn't. She didn't agree with him at all. As far as she was concerned, everything was not as it should be, and the night was far from over … and this night belonged to her.

"This night will bring balance to the world," Martel said to her and, although he was standing right beside her, his voice seemed to come from a distance. Amelia was there physically, but she'd left him in spirit. She didn't want to hear any more. This was her night and she would no longer allow anyone else to try and control it. Right or wrong Amelia would do what she felt was best.

Martel saw Amelia was distant. She was still—incredibly still. Martel was intrigued.

The hairs on the back of Amelia's neck slowly stood up in response to an energy coming from across the room. She felt someone staring at her. Martel watched her carefully and curiously as Amelia let go of his hand and turned around to find Francisco Goya, in his *Self-Portrait in the Studio,* across the room. She and the painter stared into each other's eyes and he was more alive for her than anyone she'd ever known.

She remembered describing the painting to Claude. She replayed the moment in her head, but it was as though Goya put the reminder there for her. It was as though he were pushing her toward something—as if he were another "self," belonging to her and, in looking at him, she was able to see herself through the other side of the looking glass. *In painting himself,* she'd said to Claude, *in looking in that mirror at one's self, he was unable to deny who he was. His aggression, his impulses ... the precondition of unstable thoughts and borderline madness necessary to embark on the creative process. He was bold and revealing, feared and fearful, confident and full of doubt. A pure contradiction. A man of pure art. A pure man.*

"And he was a man of no apologies," she said aloud, still only talking to herself.

"I'm sorry?" Martel said.

"How, Señor Demingo, can we expect balance in such a volatile and emotion-driven existence?" she asked in a voice Martel almost did not recognize. He said nothing. He knew it wasn't really a question, but a statement. He watched her, unaware of exactly what was happening, but able to recognize that something—from within her being—was changing, right in front of him.

Amelia closed her eyes and visualized a pentagram. The symbol began to spin clockwise, invoking her desires. Now, the music of Beethoven's "Pastoral" and her beloved husband filled her soul and guided her thoughts. As the pentagram continued to spin, it pulled in more and more of the energy surrounding her. The Witches, inside and outside, The National Gallery, could all feel something and, as the detective drew closer, he could feel something, as well—but what it was they didn't know. They didn't know that she was pulling in their energy, to strengthen her will—and neither did she—but she was becoming stronger and stronger, without making a move or a sound. She was realizing the power within herself and, as her mother had promised, that was all she needed for it to exist.

Dorian continued to watch her from across the room.

Martel was mesmerized. He finally realized what was happening. He looked at his watch—it was 11:01 p.m. He watched as the second-hand counted down the final minute and, at 11:02 p.m., he looked at Amelia and watched as she executed her moment of revenge without making one physical move. He saw it all unfold in the reflection of her eyes.

Seven black town cars, driven around Trafalgar Square by members of The Organization, were suddenly no longer under the control of their drivers. Car stereos came on and the "Pastoral" blared through the speakers of each car, at maximum volume. The drivers had no control, as the cars careened over the curbs and into the square, striking down all the men of The Organization, one at a time. All of them, but Francis Brunning.

Their wounds were hopelessly critical, but none of the men were dead and none were lucky enough to be unconscious. They felt their broken bones and crushed legs. They suffered—just as Wolfgang had—in writhing agony.

They all watched as the town cars crashed, wildly out of control, wrapping themselves around the light posts surrounding the square. The crunching of metal could be heard, almost in unison, as though they were following the notes of Amelia's own symphony of destruction.

Then all was quiet and the drivers also suffered as Wolfgang had.

The detective heard the crashes and ran to the scene. He stopped at the first car he came to, unable to see, from where he was, the massive pile-up and chaos that had taken place.

Summer and Francis had been stopped by the mayhem. Having nowhere to turn, they stood in the center of the square, Summer in horror and Francis disturbed, but excited by the force of it all—this extraordinary force, coming from just one girl.

Then Summer felt something in her chest—a sharp pain, followed by a feeling of weakness. She looked down to see that she was bleeding. It was as though she'd been stabbed—sliced from chest to abdomen—just as Grace had been, but this wound came from inside her.

Martel was speechless as he watched Amelia. She hadn't moved. He was in awe, realizing what she was doing and what was about to happen. He did nothing to stop her. It was clear that avenging her family was more important than whatever would be brought onto her by the Law of Three.

Francis watched as Summer collapsed. He stood there, as if to torture her by doing nothing, but watching her writhe in agonizing pain. She tried to ease her fall by grabbing onto the side of a fountain.

Amelia remained focused. Her eyelids slowly closed. The pentagram was still spinning, still invoking, still pulling in energy and growing.

Summer, barely breathing, raised herself on her elbow to see the havoc that had been carried out.

Amelia opened her eyes to Goya's stare—her mirror. Then she turned and walked out the door.

chapter 49

Amelia stood in the thickening fog, on the steps of The National Gallery. She looked out at the mangled town cars and bodies that littered Trafalgar Square and the surrounding streets. Members of The Organization were dead everywhere.

Amelia walked down the stairs and over to Summer, who was bleeding profusely and clearly on her deathbed. Amelia looked down at her.

Summer was relieved to see her before she died—finally, to face her with the truth of what stood between them. "At first, I hoped it wasn't true," she said. "Then, I thought, with your mother gone, I could change you, but … you are her and you carry, in you, all that the legend promised. You had no choice, but to kill me."

"And I will kill you in another life for what you've done."

"I know. It's the nature of who you are."

"You murdered my mother, my husband, and my father. You deceived me. So, yes, making you pay for that is in my nature, Summer."

"Of course it is," Jeremy said, as he slowly made his way toward Amelia with Martel's help. "Because you are, in fact, 'The One,' my dear."

Amelia turned to find Jeremy alive, but covered in blood from her attack. She was mortified by the mistake she'd made. "Jeremy, I …"

"I'll be alright. It's long, but not deep," he said. Then, he looked around at the massive destruction Amelia had caused. She followed his gaze, struck by what she had done. They were surrounded by death and suffering. "This only confirms what we always knew."

Amelia looked to Summer, now struggling with her last breaths. Then she turned back to Jeremy wanting to make sense of what was happening.

"The High Priestess gave birth to twins," he explained, "Each with equal, but opposing power."

He looked to Summer. "The children following in the bloodline of the girl—the child whom High Priestess Maeve raised— would try to balance the world with pure goodness."

Then he turned to Amelia. "And the children to follow in the bloodline of the boy—the child raised by the High Priest Domhall—would fight the Civil War of the Witches and the war against The Organization, with the necessary power. An eye for an eye. 'The One' would be the first female child, in either of those bloodlines, to reach her 28th birthday on Samhain, under the Full Blood Moon. Summer miscarried. Your mother did not."

"You can choose the other side, Amelia," Summer struggled. "You can reverse the spell. You have the power to do that, now. That's why the universe gave it to you. You're stronger than Maeve and Domhall were. You have 'The Ultimate Power'—the power to bring back balance and harmony among the Witches; to end the Civil War and stop the violent ways of your followers and The Organization."

Amelia couldn't believe what she was hearing. She began to kneel down to Summer when Jeremy pulled her back. "That is not true, Ms. Karlsen, and you know it. Balance does not always mean harmony. In fact it never does. It requires two sides and the manipulation of both. You demonstrated that, yourself, when you found you needed violence to fight your fight, didn't you? You broke your own rules daily," he said, as he put his foot over her face, preventing her from answering … and from breathing.

Summer was dead and Amelia was speechless.

"Don't blame her," Jeremy said seeing that Amelia was in shock and trying to make sense of what she was hearing. "After Summer lost her baby, it was only natural that she befriend the opposition and try to destroy the other child ... that way the coming of 'The One' would be prolonged until the dates and the planets were again in line."

Jeremy put his hand on Amelia's shoulder in a loving way, as if, for him, they were bonding. "Funny, she took such a liking to you—as if you were her own. I believe she'd hoped you weren't 'The One.' I believe she hoped to recruit you to the other side, whether you were or not."

"I'm the descendant of the son," Amelia said, almost afraid to say it out loud.

"Yes. Your blood is of the boy raised by the High Priest Domhall—by those who understood that wars must be fought, not reasoned. And all one has to do is look around to see that it's come upon you quite naturally."

Jeremy handed Amelia an envelope. "These are the missing pages from your mother's Book of Shadows. She asked me to keep them until you were ready, until you knew everything."

Amelia opened the envelope and looked at her mother's hand-writing and the passages about their linage ... She was mortified by the reality of who she was. She looked around at what she'd done, hoping that she hadn't hurt any innocent bystanders and wondering what people, the authorities and Detective Carlisle would think happened.

"It's rather magnificent," Jeremy said, like a proud father. "Don't worry, darling Amelia. The only difference between good and evil and right and wrong is perception."

Amelia looked to Martel for a glimmer of hope, but instead saw him for what he truly was—a self-proclaimed Witch and man of great evil.

The three of them stood in the fog, taking in what surrounded them, when they heard footsteps slowly approaching. It was too dark and the fog was too heavy for them to see who it was. Then, before anyone realized what was happening, someone shot Jeremy and Martel in the back. When their bodies dropped, she saw that Francis was holding the gun. He stood, facing Amelia, and smiled.

He handed her a rock. "Perception can be one of life's greatest horrors, don't you agree?" Amelia didn't say anything. Francis nodded and continued walking across the square and away from the scene. Amelia watched as he joined Dorian and they both disappeared into the night.

She looked down at the rock. It was the same unique rock she had dropped in the fountain at the Japanese Tea Gardens in San Francisco when she was seven-years-old. The sounds of Beethoven's "Pastoral" filled her mind. Then, through the fog, they appeared— Amelia's Witch and Wiccan enemies and followers surrounded Trafalgar Square, staring at her and the path of destruction she'd left, wondering what the future would bring.

Among them, in the distance, was Detective Carlisle. He'd finally realized ... he'd realized that it was Amelia's birthday and that "The One" was not a fairy tale at all. He knew that the slaughter was her doing. That it was payback. And that she was an anomaly who could not be changed, and could not be challenged, and could not be harmed ... but still, all he wanted to do was to save her— but from what he wasn't sure.

Amelia looked down into one of the fountains, but her view was not of what was actually there. She found herself looking down into the view from the top of the bridge in the Japanese Tea Garden. She watched as the final ripples, from the first rock she dropped so many years ago, smoothed out over water. Her day-time view turned to night and she returned to the currrent images of Trafalgar Square.

Amelia's reflection appeared over that of the Full Blood Moon. Her image was translucent black over the imposing orange and red ball. The detective watched as she held the rock high up over the water, then opened her hand and let it fall.

"Amelia!" the detective screamed. Amelia looked up and saw him running toward her. And all he saw was tragedy in her bright green eyes, now that she held the key to the world's most powerful magick. Amelia heard the splash of the rock hitting the water and looked down. A pentagram appeared where the rock hit. Blood poured down over the reflection of the moon and Amelia, and the pentagram began to spin. Amelia stood watching the water, as hundreds of Witches stood watching her, and the ambulances and policemen began to arrive, and the detective stood at a loss while Francis Brunning and Dorian Caldwell warmed themselves by a fire, determining their next move against the now totally alone, Amelia Pivens Kreutzer, "The One."

The End

Printed in the United States
110495LV00004B/1-96/P